TOWER
OF THE
FIVE ORDERS

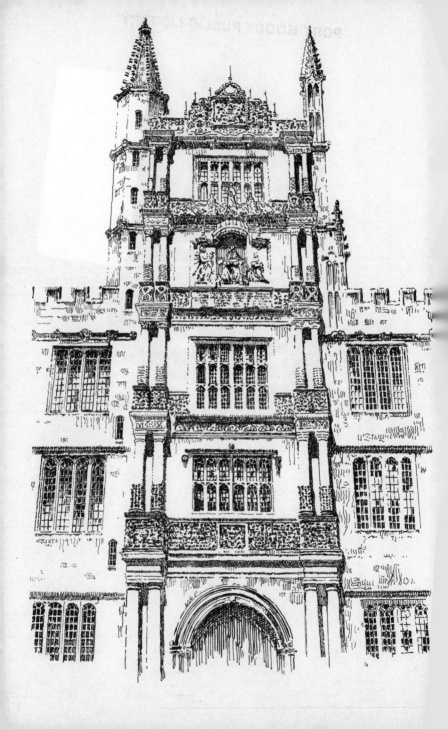

TOWER OF THE FIVE ORDERS

BY DERON R. HICKS

ILLUSTRATED BY MARK EDWARD GEYER

HOUGHTON MIFFLIN HARCOURT
BOSTON NEW YORK

www.hmhco.com

The text of this book is set in New Century Schoolbook.
The illustrations are pen and ink.
Book design by Carol Chu

The Library of Congress has cataloged the
hardcover edition as follows:
Hicks, Deron R.
Tower of the Five Orders / by Deron R. Hicks ;
illustrations by Mark Geyer.
pages cm. — (The Shakespeare Mysteries ; book 2)
Sequel to: Secrets of Shakespeare's grave.
Summary: Thirteen-year-old Colophon Letterford and her cousin Julian
continue their quest to uncover their family's treasure as new clues lead them
to Oxford, England, seeking to unravel a connection to Christopher Marlowe.
[1. Mystery and detective stories. 2. Adventure and adventurers—Fiction. 3.
Marlowe, Christopher, 1564–1593—Fiction. 4. Shakespeare, William, 1564–
1616—Fiction. 5. Cousins—Fiction. 6. Family-owned business enterprises—
Fiction. 7. Oxford (England)—Fiction. 8. England—Fiction.] I. Geyer, Mark, ill.
II. Hicks, Deron R. Secrets of Shakespeare's grave. III. Title.
PZ7.H531615Tow   2013
[Fic]—dc23
2012045195

ISBN: 978-0-547-83953-0 hardcover
ISBN: 978-0-544-33630-8 paperback

Manufactured in the United States of America
DOC 10 9 8 7 6 5 4 3 2 1

4500494136

TO MAGGIE.
WE MISS
YOU.

Contents

PART II

PART I

"I hold the Fates bound fast in iron chains,
And with my hand turn Fortune's wheel about."

Christopher Marlowe, *Tamburlaine the Great* (1588)

Prologue

Elanor Bull's Public House
Deptford, England
May 30, 1593

The smell of roasted meat and the noisy clank of kitchen pots filled the room. A young potboy whistled as he gathered dishes from a table and shuffled them off to the back of the house.

Christopher Marlowe gazed out the window at the rapidly fading sunlight. He took a long draw from his tankard of ale, closed his eyes, and savored the brief moment of peace. It had been, to say the least, a bad year. The plague had once again cast a spell of death across London. In an effort to slow its progress, by order of the Crown, the theaters had been closed. As if the loss of his livelihood was not sufficient, Marlowe had—in just the previous month—been arrested, charged with heresy, and forbidden to leave the city until called upon for trial.

Marlowe was not a fool. He knew that the trial would be a mere formality. It was clear that forces were aligned against him—the same forces that had once called upon his assistance. The charge of heresy was utter nonsense. Facts, however, were of no consequence. He would be lucky to escape a date with the executioner's sword. Two days earlier it had seemed all but certain that he would spend the remaining days of his life in shackles and under guard. And yet for some reason, he had been allowed to remain at liberty until the time for his trial.

Odd, Marlowe thought as he took another drink from his tankard. *The Crown is usually not so . . .*

He paused in midthought.

Fie! What a fool I am. Of course they let me go.

He contemplated the obvious: that they had never intended to provide him a trial. He knew far too much—his fate had already been decided.

I shall leave for France forthwith.

Marlowe started to rise from his seat when he noticed that the room had suddenly turned silent. No banging of pots in the kitchen. No scuffing of chairs along the stone floor. No murmur of conversation.

Nothing.

Marlowe peered around the room. It was empty. Elanor Bull, who owned and operated the public house, was nowhere to be seen. The potboy's whistle was silent. Marlowe had been so absorbed in his own thoughts that he had failed to notice what was taking place around him.

Fie again!

He set his tankard on the table, and his hand went instantly to the dagger at his side. The front door creaked open. Marlowe shielded his eyes from the light of the late afternoon sun as it streamed through the open doorway. He could not see who had entered or how many.

When the door shut, a large man dressed in black turned to face him. He held a sword at his side. Two men stood beside the man in black—their swords drawn.

"Robert Poley," said Marlowe to the man standing at the door. "What news? Have ye come on behalf of God, the Crown, or the Devil?"

Poley spoke slowly, his voice deep and raspy.

"Neither God nor the Crown has any use for thee, Christopher Marlowe."

"Aye, 'tis true, Robert Poley," Marlowe replied, "but I suspect that it is on the Devil's behalf that a man such as yourself was sent."

Marlowe held the dagger close to his hip as he stood and moved toward the center of the room. He needed time to assess the situation. "So the Earl of Essex prefers his secrets in the grave?" he said.

Poley grunted and spat on the floor. "Impertinent dog," he growled. "'Tis worms who shall bear witness to what secrets ye hold."

Marlowe knew that there was a rear door leading to a narrow alley behind the tavern. He could make it to the alley before Poley and his men had time to react. But he also knew Poley—he would have the exit covered. The only way out would be through the front door and at the point of his own dagger. Marlowe cursed himself for lack of more substantial arms.

At that moment, Marlowe heard a faint shuffle of feet in the darkness behind him.

He smiled. *Clumsy fool.*

Marlowe pivoted backwards just as a sword thrust at him from the shadows. His dagger flashed from his side and into the right arm of his attacker. The man screamed as the sword fell from his hand and clanked onto the hard stone floor. Marlowe grabbed the sword and turned to face Poley and his henchmen. He grinned as he ran the steel of his dagger down the blade of the sword. "Ye may seek to whet thy swords on my bones," he said, "but ye will find me a most unwilling grindstone."

"So be it," growled Poley.

The clank of steel on steel rang through the room and into the street beyond.

CHAPTER ONE

Auspicious

Auspicious—Presenting favorable circumstances
or showing signs of a favorable outcome.

The discovery of the Shakespeare manuscripts by
Colophon Letterford and her cousin Julian did not
go unnoticed. Universally hailed as the most important literary discovery of the last century, if not of all
time, the story seized the public's imagination.

The *New York Times* ran a five-part series about
the discovery. The *Boston Globe* featured a picture
of Mull Letterford, Colophon's father, on the front
page of its Sunday edition. An editorial in *Le Monde*

praised the Letterford family and their contributions to literary history.

Magazines such as *Time, Newsweek, National Geographic,* and *Bon Appétit* profiled the discovery with cover stories.

Mull Letterford was interviewed on NPR, CNN, Fox, CBS, NBC, ABC, the BBC, the CBC, CCTV, and Radio Liechtenstein. Colophon was invited to the set of *MythBusters*—her all-time favorite TV show —and celebrated her thirteenth birthday with the cast and crew. Julian appeared on *Good Morning America.* It was the first time Colophon had ever seen him with his hair combed and his face shaved —and wearing a tie.

The academic community—which could barely contain its collective glee—geared up for what was anticipated to be years of research, examination, interpretation, and explication of the manuscripts. Requests poured in to Letterford & Sons from re-searchers for opportunities to study the original manuscripts. Every reputable (and not so reputable) Shakespearean scholar on the planet offered his or her services free of charge just for the opportunity to have access to the manuscripts. Preorders for the summer edition of the *Shakespeare Quarterly* overwhelmed the limited staff and resources of the Johns Hopkins University Press. Meg Letterford, Colophon's mother, received invitations from across the academic spectrum to join faculties as a visiting professor. The Folger Shakespeare Library in Washington, D.C., held a symposium that coincided with a week-long exhibit of several of the manuscripts. Tickets for the exhibit sold out in minutes.

Numerous offers were made to purchase the manuscripts, for stunning amounts. But Mull Letterford held firm. The manuscripts, he said repeatedly, belonged to humanity. He could not bear the thought of them ending up in the private collection of some billionaire, never to be studied or enjoyed by the rest of the world.

The Letterford name, well known and respected within literary circles for centuries, had now become well known and respected in the world at large.

It was a glorious time.

And it was short-lived.

CHAPTER TWO

Exposure

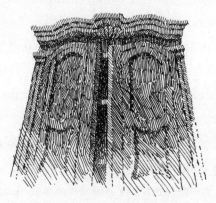

Exposure—An instance of being subjected
to an action or an influence; revelation,
especially of crime or guilt.

Carbondale, Pennsylvania
Secure-Tite Specialty Storage
Tuesday, April 17
2:05 p.m.

"Unit number?"

"Two hundred thirty-five."

"Name in which the unit is registered?"

"Reginald Whitmore."

"Identification, please."

Whitmore placed his driver's license into the sliding drawer and pushed the drawer back under the inch-thick bulletproof glass. The clerk checked the identification, entered some information into the computer, and returned the license.

"Please enter your code on the keypad," the clerk said.

Whitmore punched in his five-digit code. The light on the keypad turned green.

"Thank you, Mr. Whitmore," the clerk replied as the secure door opened.

Whitmore picked up his briefcase and stepped through the doorway. He walked to the elevator and pressed the call button. He did not mind the security precautions. To the contrary, that was one of the primary reasons he had selected this particular facility. Security, however, was only one of its aspects that had interested him. The facility served a specialized clientele—antique dealers, art collectors, and anyone else who needed to store delicate items of value under proper conditions. The entire facility was maintained at a constant temperature of seventy-two degrees and a humidity level of fifty percent. Its fire-suppression system was based on foam, not water. The facility's owners understood that antique tables and ancient oil paintings do not respond well to a dousing of water. The air was recirculated at least twice a day through specialized filters that removed any trace of airborne contaminants that might damage the precious items stored within.

The elevator pinged and the door opened. Whitmore stepped in and pushed the button for the second floor. The trip took less than five seconds. Once the elevator door opened, Whitmore stepped out, turned right, and headed to unit 235. Upon reaching it, he punched a code into the keypad adjacent to the unit's door.

There was a slight pause, then . . . *click click click*.

The door unlocked. Whitmore stepped inside, turned on the light, and shut the door.

Another short pause, then . . . *click click click*.

The door was secure once again.

Whitmore looked around the room. Several pieces of antique furniture were arranged neatly against the walls. One particular piece towered over the rest —an early-eighteenth-century armoire. Heavy and thick, it stood at least eight feet tall and six feet wide. It seemed impossibly deep. Made of chestnut, the wood glowed with a patina that could have been achieved only by centuries of care and use. Whitmore walked over to the armoire and opened wide its large doors.

He stood back and admired his collection.

It had taken years to assemble: pages from illuminated manuscripts, old maps, papyrus scrolls, and rare books that had languished for far too long on forgotten shelves. His position allowed him access to some of the most prestigious libraries and collections of ancient books and manuscripts across the globe. Access had been important. Patience, however, had been the true key to building his collection.

Don't get greedy, he had told himself frequently. And he had not.

He had passed on opportunities to add many, many items to his collection. And his patience had paid off. The opportunities inevitably presented themselves. People were lazy, sloppy, and easily distracted.

And they trusted him.

After all these years, no one suspected. Not a single librarian. Not a single curator. Not a single collector.

No one.

His acquisition process was decidedly low tech but effective: wait until no one was paying attention, then simply slip the book, manuscript, or map into the hidden compartment in his briefcase. Using this process, he had built an impressive collection. But it had its limits. He would never be a member of the Roxburghe Club. His collection would never rival many of the private collections held across the globe. Put together by kings, industrialists, and tyrants, those collections were symbols of power and wealth—nothing more. His collection would always pale in comparison.

Whitmore grinned. *Until now.*

Now, he thought, *I have something that only one other person on the planet has.*

Whitmore opened his briefcase, pulled out a large aluminum notebook, and placed it on a small table next to the armoire. He opened the notebook to reveal a single document. He took a pair of tweezers from a drawer and carefully lifted the fragile document. He placed it on a piece of green felt on the table.

Magnificent.

This single page, he knew, would be the crowning jewel of any collection—an actual page from a manuscript in William Shakespeare's own hand. He relished the thought of all the collectors, libraries, and curators who would give anything—pay anything—to have the document that now lay in front of him.

And then the phone rang.

Whitmore looked around, confused. He always set his cell phone on vibrate. Had he somehow forgotten?

His hand instantly went to his belt, where he kept his phone.

It wasn't vibrating. And it certainly wasn't ringing.

He looked around in horror. The phone rang again.

The sound was coming from the armoire.

Whitmore made his way over to the armoire and looked inside. The phone rang again.

The sound appeared to be coming from the uppermost shelf. He reached up and felt along the tops of the books. His hand came across a small metallic object—completely out of place atop vellum-covered books from the fifteenth and sixteenth centuries. He grabbed the object and pulled it down.

He held in his hand a small cell phone. A phone that was not his. A phone that he had not placed on the shelf.

It rang again.

How is this happening?

The phone rang again.

This isn't possible.

The phone rang again.

No one knows about this place.

No one.

But, he suddenly realized, someone did.

The phone rang again.

He had no choice—he had to answer it. Whitmore pushed the button, closed his eyes, and held it up to his right ear.

"Hello?"

"Good afternoon, Dr. Whitmore," a voice responded. "How is the collection coming along? Quite an impressive new addition you've obtained, isn't it?" The voice was pleasant and conversational.

Whitmore's heart froze. His voice cracked as he spoke. "I'm sorry, what are you talking about? What collection? I think you have the wrong number."

The voice laughed. "Come now, Dr. Whitmore, please don't take me for a fool. Your collection is very impressive. I enjoyed looking through it."

"What do you want?" Whitmore asked.

"Merely a favor—nothing more."

Whitmore sat and listened as the voice told him what it wanted him to do.

"I truly appreciate your assistance in this endeavor," the voice concluded.

"I have no choice," Whitmore replied.

The tone of the voice immediately changed. It was no longer pleasant, but cold and flat. "Correct," it responded, "you have no choice."

✢ ✢ ✢

Trigue James ended the phone call.

Whitmore would cooperate.

James had known that he would.

James was parked a half mile away from the entrance to the storage facility, at a small strip mall. It provided a perfect vantage point. He could observe anyone who entered or exited.

James took a sip from a bottle of Diet Coke. Treemont contacting him a month ago had come as somewhat of a surprise. Things had not gone well in London the previous December, and James had been reluctant to have any further involvement with Treemont's schemes.

But Treemont had been persistent—he had insisted that he needed James's unique skills. Persistence, James knew all too well, could be a sign of impatience—and an impatient client was a risky client.

He took another sip of Diet Coke.

Treemont, however, had not struck James as impatient or risky. So James had offered his services yet again—for a substantially increased price. After all, a job was a job.

James glanced at the storage facility. Whitmore's car still sat in the parking lot.

He opened the back of his cell phone and carefully removed the SIM card. He snapped it in two, then dropped both pieces into the half-empty bottle of Diet Coke.

James started his car, pulled out of the strip mall, and headed east.

Manchester, Georgia
Friday, May 25
6:15 a.m.

Colophon Letterford sat upright in bed as soon as her alarm sounded.

It was the last day of school.

Normally Colophon dreaded those words. She enjoyed school. She enjoyed her teachers and her classes (particularly social studies) and seeing her friends every day. Not that summer was entirely bad—it had its brief moments of fun. But it usually brought something that Colophon dreaded.

Summer camp.

She hated summer camp.

Each June for the last three years she had been shipped off for four agonizingly long weeks at Camp

Oglethorpe in North Carolina. Her father had attended Camp Oglethorpe in his youth and frequently regaled her with stories of summers spent swimming in the lake, learning to fish, canoeing, making crafts, and engaging in a host of other fun camp activities.

He had obviously been brainwashed.

In Colophon's opinion, Camp Oglethorpe was a mosquito-infested chamber of horrors where the temperature never dropped below one hundred degrees. And that wasn't even the worst part. Colophon had never been among the most popular girls at camp. She always had one or two good friends and had always gotten along reasonably well with most of the other kids there. But the camp was run by a small cadre of popular kids. Every year Colophon expected it to change, but it didn't. The popular kids got the best camp assignments, the best cabins, the best table in the cafeteria, and the coolest counselors. The divide between the popular kids and the rest of the campers (which included Colophon) was huge. And it was dreadful.

But maybe this summer would be different. This year it wouldn't matter who the popular kids were, how hot it got, or if the mosquitoes were the size of small cars. Colophon had solved an ancient family riddle, barely escaped with her life from an underground crypt, chased a criminal through the streets of London, and helped save the family business. Compared to all that, Camp Oglethorpe would be a minor challenge.

She dressed quickly, brushed her teeth, and hurried downstairs to the kitchen.

"Good morning, Coly," Audrey Letterford said as Colophon entered the kitchen.

"Aunt Audrey! What are you doing here?"

"Your father called me late last night and asked me to come down and take you and Case to school this morning. He had . . . something come up."

Mull Letterford's older sister was a fixture in the Letterford home, so Colophon was not particularly surprised to find her in the kitchen. Meg Letterford was in San Francisco at an academic conference, so Colophon's father had planned to take her and Case to school that morning. Still, something seemed off with her aunt. She was not displaying her usual room-consuming personality.

"Is something wrong?" asked Colophon. "You seem . . . upset."

"I'm just tired, dear," her aunt replied. "I didn't get in from Atlanta until early this morning."

Colophon decided not to pursue the subject. It was not the first time her father had had to rush away on business. And her aunt did look tired—exhausted even.

Case managed to make his way downstairs at 6:43 a.m., which was precisely two minutes before they had to leave for school. He took one look at his aunt, grunted hello, grabbed a can of iced coffee from the refrigerator, and went out to the car.

The drive to school was quiet. Case slept the entire way. Despite Colophon's best efforts to engage her aunt in conversation, Audrey barely spoke.

When Audrey dropped Colophon off at the middle school, Colophon reminded her that it was the last day of school and that she would be getting out at noon. "Don't forget me," she joked.

Audrey simply nodded. "I'll see you then."

Colophon stood on the sidewalk and watched the car pull off toward the high school. Aunt Audrey had seemed on the verge of tears. Colophon would have to get to the bottom of whatever was bothering her aunt later, when she picked her up.

Colophon turned and headed down the covered walkway to the middle school building. She didn't need any books for the last day of class, and she had already cleaned out her locker for the year, so she headed straight for homeroom. Every classroom in the building buzzed with the excitement of the last day of school. As Colophon turned the corner into her homeroom, she could hear the loud chatter of her classmates.

But the chatter ceased as soon as Colophon entered. Every eye turned toward her.

What was going on?

Colophon slowly made her way up the row toward her desk. As she walked, she looked over at her best friend at school, Ashley Eager, who sat a couple of rows away. Ashley quickly averted her eyes and looked down at her desk. Colophon glanced around the classroom. Ms. Bowman, her teacher, was nowhere to be found.

Colophon reached her desk and sat down. The room was absolutely silent. At the next desk over sat Elliott Messer.

"Elliott," she said, "what's going on?"

He tried to ignore her.

"Elliott," she repeated, "what's going on?"

He turned to her and whispered: "Ms. Bowman told us not to say anything."

"Anything about what?" she whispered back.

"Go ahead, Elliott," said Anna Drew, who sat in front of Colophon. "Show it to her."

Elliott handed Colophon a folded-up newspaper. "I'm sorry," he said.

Colophon opened the newspaper—it was the morning edition of the *Columbus Ledger*. The headline, which covered half the front page, read: SHAKESPEARE MANUSCRIPTS FAKE.

Colophon stared at the headline. She could feel every eye in the room on her. No one spoke.

Then she felt a hand on her shoulder. It was Ms. Bowman.

"Coly," the teacher said, "I'm so sorry. I was in the front hallway looking for you. You must've slipped by in the crowd."

Colophon couldn't respond. Her eyes burned. She was on the verge of tears.

"Your father just called," she continued. "Your aunt is coming back to pick you up."

Colophon simply stared at the headline.

Colophon sat on a couch in the principal's office and read the article. According to the newspaper, a professor by the name of Reginald Whitmore had announced with great fanfare that the Shakespeare manuscripts were, in all likelihood, forgeries. Dr. Whitmore, who specialized in the analysis of sixteenth- and seventeenth-century manuscripts and books, had actually been hired by Letterford & Sons to assist in the cataloging and analysis of the manuscripts. "I have significant concerns over the authenticity of the paper, the ink, and the handwriting on the documents," Dr. Whitmore had said. "These documents should be subjected to the highest level of scrutiny and require extensive evaluation." A representative from the British Museum had suggested that a commission be established to authenticate the documents.

"Coly."

It was Case. He stood in the doorway of the principal's office. His hair was a mess, and he had a bruised lower lip.

"What happened to you?" she asked.

"Someone in my homeroom class thought it was a good idea to express his opinion about the manuscripts."

"Dad's going to freak when he sees you."

"I think Dad has other things on his mind." Case sat down beside his sister on the couch.

"The manuscripts are real," Colophon said. "You'll see—Dad will prove they're real."

Case sighed. "I hope you're right, Coly. I really hope you're right."

CHAPTER THREE
Pedant

Pedant—one who pays undue attention
to minor details or formal rules.

British Library
London, England
Wednesday, May 30
10:28 a.m.

Mull Letterford sat in a small and uncomfortable
chair in a small and uncomfortable waiting room

within the administrative wing of the British Library. The waiting room served several offices, including the office of one P. Mallory Fullingham-Trout, MSW. Mull glanced at his watch. His appointment with Mr. Fullingham-Trout was scheduled for 10:30.

The last few days had been a blur. The previous Thursday he had received a late-afternoon phone call about a press conference that was to be held in New York City that evening. The press conference had been called by Dr. Reginald Whitmore—the man Mull had hired to help curate the Shakespeare manuscripts. Dr. Whitmore apparently now questioned the authenticity of the documents and had actually suggested that they might be forgeries. The news had stunned Mull. Dr. Whitmore had received unlimited access to the manuscripts and had never expressed a single concern or doubt over their authenticity—until now.

Upon receiving news of the press conference, Mull had called his sister in Atlanta and asked if she would come down and take care of Colophon and Case. He had arrived in New York early Friday morning—just in time to read the morning's headlines.

SHAKESPEARE SHENANIGANS! read the *New York Post*.

MANUSCRIPT MISCHIEF! cried the *Daily News.*

WAS SHAKESPEARE REALLY ELVIS? questioned the *National Enquirer.*

Mull had spent most of the early morning fending off the press. He became so caught up in responding to the media that it did not occur to him until it was too late that Case and Colophon were on their way to school and knew nothing of the news. His anxious calls to the school and to his sister were too late.

Later on Friday, a representative of the British government had contacted him, asking him to be available for a meeting this morning at the British Library. So he had flown to London and now sat waiting for that meeting to begin.

The door to Mr. Fullingham-Trout's office opened precisely at 10:30, and a short, thin man with thick glasses stepped into the waiting room.

"Good morning, Mr. Letterford, I'm Mallory Fullingham-Trout. Won't you please come in?"

Mull gathered his documents and entered the small, cramped office. Fullingham-Trout motioned for him to take a seat in a small chair in front of the desk, then settled into the large leather chair behind the desk.

"May I offer you some tea?"

"No, thank you," replied Mull.

"Very well. I would like to begin by thanking you for being here this morning. As you can imagine, the DCMS was very excited when the Shakespeare manuscripts were discovered last year—"

"The DCMS?" asked Mull.

"The Department for Culture, Media and Sport." Fullingham-Trout seemed perturbed that Mull had not recognized the acronym. "To my point," he continued, "the department was very excited by the discovery of the manuscripts."

"As we all were," said Mull.

Fullingham-Trout cleared his throat. "Yes, I suppose you were. But now we have this . . . um . . . shall we say, complication."

"The manuscripts are real," Mull said bluntly. He had held the fragile manuscripts in his hands. He had read the handwritten notes and stage directions that could have come from only one man. He had no doubts.

Fullingham-Trout cleared his throat again. "Yes, yes, that would be quite wonderful, wouldn't it? The Crown, as you are well aware, took great pride in this discovery. Not everyone gets to meet the queen, do they? But we can't simply ignore Dr. Whitmore's allegations. After all, he worked for you, did he not?"

Mull nodded.

"Very well," said Fullingham-Trout. "The minister for DCMS, through his under secretary, has asked me to seek your cooperation in addressing this matter."

"I'll certainly cooperate in any way necessary."

The short, thin man beamed. "Excellent, excellent. We have already started the process of putting together a commission to review the manuscripts. The chairman of the commission will be Sir Hedley Penrose."

"I'm not familiar with Sir Penrose," said Mull.

"A good man, I assure you," replied Fullingham-Trout. "Sir Penrose honorably served the Crown for forty years as a valued civil servant. As good a bureaucrat as there ever has been. He was well known for his thorough reports—an absolute model of government efficiency. You may have heard of his West Upton Sewer Report?"

Mull shook his head. "Sorry, no."

Fullingham-Trout seemed disappointed. "Pity. Rest assured, it was the best seven hundred pages on sewer financing that I've ever read.

"Anyway," he continued, "I have been personally assured by Sir Penrose that the commission will be very comprehensive in its efforts."

"And how long do you anticipate it will take?" asked Mull.

"Oh, it should move along quite swiftly, I imagine," replied Fullingham-Trout. "A committee has been set up to review the qualifications of proposed commission members. Once the committee has issued its report, the minister will act quickly to appoint the commission—after, of course, the committee's report is reviewed by the DCMS Standing Panel on Committee Reports. Once that report has been approved and reviewed, I believe we will have the full commission appointed in no more than four or five months."

Mull sat upright in his chair. "Four or five months just to appoint the commission?"

Fullingham-Trout beamed with pride. "Yes, I was surprised as well at how quickly the process will move. Normally it would take at least a year. But the minister has insisted that we move this process along as quickly as possible."

Mull could barely bring himself to ask the next question. "And how long do you anticipate that it will take for the commission to reach its conclusion?"

Fullingham-Trout puffed out his chest. His eyes filled his thick glasses. "Oh, rest assured, Mr. Letterford, Sir Penrose has personally assured me that he will push to complete the commission's report in no more than two years."

Mull sank back into his seat.

Letterford & Sons would not survive for two years.

Atlanta, Georgia
Thursday, May 31
4:35 p.m.

Mull turned on his cell phone as soon as his plane landed. The text messages immediately started pinging. They were all from Uncle Portis.

The first message read: *Family has requested meeting.*

The second read: *Meeting scheduled for 5:00 p.m. at the Atlanta office.*

Mull walked into the main conference room of Letterford & Sons a few minutes after five. He looked and felt exhausted. Treemont sat at the far end of the conference room table. Uncle Portis escorted Mull to a chair opposite him.

This time, as had not been the case at the meeting the previous Thanksgiving, Treemont was silent. Today Brantley Letterford—a distant cousin of Mull's—stood and addressed the family. Brantley expressed concern over Mull's ability to lead Letterford & Sons under the current circumstances. The media, he noted, were openly suggesting that the Shakespeare manuscripts might be forgeries.

"Is that what you believe?" asked Mull. "That the manuscripts are forgeries? That I would place the reputation of this company in jeopardy?"

Brantley avoided Mull's gaze. "My opinion is of little consequence," he muttered. "But your owner-ship of the company rested upon the authenticity of those manuscripts—and that authenticity is now in question."

Mull glared across the table at Brantley. It was true that the timely discovery of the Shakespeare manuscripts had allowed Mull to remain the owner of Letterford & Sons. If Colophon had not uncovered and followed the clue hidden in the portrait of Miles Letterford, Treemont would now be the firm's owner. But Mull also knew that Treemont's treachery and scheming were the reasons his ownership of the com-pany had ever been questioned in the first place. And despite all appearances, Mull knew that Treemont was also behind today's meeting. Brantley had al-ways been a bit of a weasel, but he was a follower and nothing more. He would never have called this meeting on his own accord or spoken with such confi-dence. Treemont was clearly in charge. But who else was involved? And why?

Brantley argued that the condition of the company

had to be carefully monitored and assessed—and that immediate damage control was required. He suggested that another family member should be selected to take on this task—someone who was not tied to the discovery of the now-disputed manuscripts. Treemont, Brantley explained, was uniquely qualified. Treemont's father, now deceased, had been a loyal and respected employee of the company for many, many years. Treemont had practically grown up in the business.

Uncle Portis stood and addressed the family. He agreed that Treemont's *father* had been a very loyal employee. He insisted, however, that change was not needed—the manuscripts would be proven authentic. Everyone simply needed to be patient.

"Patience will not repair the reputation of this company," replied Brantley. "It is time for action."

Mull looked around the table. Clearly the decision had been made long before he entered the room. A quick vote was taken among the family members. Drained of any desire to fight, Mull simply nodded his assent.

Chapter Four
Hint

Hint—A slight indication or intimation.

Manchester, Georgia
Friday, June 1
9:35 a.m.

Colophon put the ancient inkwell up to her left eye and stared through the dark glass at the morning sun. Her father had given her the inkwell as a memento of her efforts in discovering the Shakespeare manuscripts.

"Truth be told," Mull had said, "this should be in a museum somewhere. After all, it may very well have belonged to Shakespeare himself."

He had paused.

"But there is no one on this planet who deserves this more than you."

He had placed the inkwell in her hand and lightly kissed her forehead. It had been a sign of trust and love.

Colophon flopped back onto her bed and cradled the inkwell against her chest.

Treemont! She just knew he was behind all this.

Worst of all, Treemont would now be sitting in Atlanta overlooking and interfering with everything her father did. It was all so frustrating and infuriating. And she felt powerless to help.

She rolled over in bed and stared at the inkwell.

Too bad it didn't say "Property of William Shakespeare"—that would prove the manuscripts were real.

She turned the inkwell over in her hands. The bottle was rather unremarkable: dark glass with a black metal cap.

Certainly doesn't look fancy enough for the world's most famous author, she thought.

Just then the morning light briefly glinted across the cap. As it did, a strange pattern emerged—and just as quickly disappeared.

She pulled over her bedside lamp, turned it on,

and shoved the cap under the bright light. She slowly rotated it under the light until . . .

Words. There were *words* on the cap!

Colophon rubbed the cap with her shirt in an effort to remove some of the dark tarnish. It didn't work. Whatever was there remained faint and illegible.

She popped out of her bed, raced down the stairs, and headed straight to the kitchen. She threw open the cabinet under the sink and sifted through the various cleaners.

It's here somewhere.

"Gotcha!" she exclaimed. In her hand, Colophon held a small bottle of Archa-Nu Silver Polish. She grabbed a dry washcloth from the linen closet and applied a small dab of polish to the cap. She allowed it to dry, then carefully rubbed out the hazy coating. The first cleaning removed a great deal of tarnish, but the cap remained impossible to read. She applied another dab of polish and waited, then rubbed it off.

She gasped.

It wasn't just words. There was more—an engraving of some sort. But the cap was still too dark to determine exactly what the engraving was.

She quickly applied another dab of polish and rubbed it off.

And another.

And another.

And then finally, there it was.

On the top of the cap was a coat of arms—faint but distinct. It consisted of a shield divided into four sections. In the top-left and bottom-right sections was what appeared to be. . . . a bird of some sort.

In the top-right and bottom-left sections were three flowers.

And directly below the shield were five words: QVOD ME NVTRIT ME DESTRVIT.

Colophon sat on the kitchen floor and stared at the cap. Was this the evidence that would prove that the manuscripts were really written by Shakespeare?

She bolted to her feet, grabbed her phone, and started to dial her father's cell phone number.

And then it hit her.

If she gave this information to her father, he would turn it over to the commission investigating the manuscripts. That would, after all, be the right thing to do. And her father always did the right thing.

But we can't wait two years.

Treemont won't wait two years.

Colophon put the phone down.

No, she concluded, it was up to her to figure this out. Again.

Case sat on the edge of his bed and studied the cap of the inkwell intently. He turned it over several times in his hands, held it up to the light, and ran his index finger across the engraving. "You have no idea what this means," he finally said.

"It's Latin," replied Colophon. "It means 'that which nourishes me destroys me.' I looked it up."

He rolled his eyes. "That's not what I meant," he said. "I know it's Latin." He held up the inkwell. "You know what it says, but you don't know what it really means."

He was right, and Colophon hated it when he was right.

Case handed the inkwell to his sister. "You know you can't do this alone."

"Maybe I can," she replied.

"No, maybe you can't. You're barely thirteen years old. You can't even leave the house without permission. And I don't know anything about Latin inscriptions on ancient inkwells. We need help."

Colophon sighed. He was right. Again.

CHAPTER FIVE
Perusal

Perusal—Reading or examining,
typically with great care.

Hay-on-Wye
Wales, United Kingdom
Friday, June 1
2:52 p.m.

Two small hazy windows and a narrow wooden door
adorned the first story of the building that stood

unimpressively at the bottom of Castle Street. The sign hanging above the door read simply BOOKS.

It would have been easy to pass by the store with little notice, and several months ago Julian had almost done just that. Hay-on-Wye, after all, was filled with any number of large and impressive bookstores, with rooms and rooms of ancient books and manuscripts. And it was those very bookstores that had drawn Julian to this small Welsh town on the border with England. The town boasted more than forty bookstores—almost one for every fifty residents.

He was looking for a book that might help him uncover the secret to the symbol he was researching—the symbol that he believed held the key to the real Letterford family treasure. But what book? Julian wasn't entirely sure. He had searched high and low in bookstores and libraries throughout the United Kingdom. He just knew the answer was out there somewhere. And this little bookstore on Castle Street? It hardly seemed worth the effort.

And then he hesitated.

It might be worth a few minutes of his time to look around inside.

And so three months ago Julian had walked into the little bookstore at the bottom of Castle Street.

The simple little bookstore, it turned out, occupied

two stories, a full basement and a deep subbasement —all filled from floor to ceiling with books. The store itself occupied almost the entire block. It was cavernous, dark, dusty, and dim. It did not offer coffee, lattes, scones, Wi-Fi, comfy chairs, magazines, or any other amenity. It simply had books—and a lot of them.

As Julian quickly learned, however, the proprietor of this particular bookstore—a small hunched woman by the name of Adda Craddock—was far more adept at acquiring books than she was at maintaining them in any semblance of order. Although she had shelved the books under general categories such as history, religion, and travel, the sheer volume on any particular subject rendered those categories useless. History books occupied an entire floor and were not otherwise divided into themes, periods, or subcategories. As far as Ms. Craddock was concerned, history was simply history.

She roamed among her books constantly, claiming to have some notion as to where certain books might or might not be. In his first trip to the bookstore, Julian had requested her assistance in locating books on symbols, particularly volumes from the sixteenth or seventeenth century. He had explained that he was looking for anything that might help him understand the significance of the symbol for the Greek letter sigma—Σ.

Julian had been obsessing over the subject of symbols ever since the discovery of the Shakespeare manuscripts the previous Christmas. In particular, he obsessed over the symbol for sigma engraved on the box in which the manuscripts had been found. No one else—not even Colophon—had seemed to notice the symbol. Others had simply taken it for granted. The family had been far too excited about the manuscripts. But the symbol concerned Julian. It was clear that it represented more than just ownership of the family business.

The manuscripts, he was convinced, were not the true treasure. They were simply another step in the quest. The symbol, he hoped, would provide the answer.

Ms. Craddock had assured Julian that she had at least three books on symbology and, true to her word, located them within a few minutes. He was impressed. Unfortunately, the books did not contain the information he was seeking. Ms. Craddock, however, promised to keep an eye out for any more books and to let Julian know if she found anything.

And find books she had.

Three times over the course of the next three

months, Julian had traveled to Ms. Craddock's shop to review large stacks of dusty books that were related in some way to symbols. However, notwithstanding the bookstore proprietor's diligent efforts, this had proven to be a time-consuming approach. Hay-on-Wye was not the easiest place to reach. And the volumes had failed to provide any new insights into the symbol on the box. Julian had given up hope of finding anything of value in Ms. Craddock's store—when he received a letter from her informing him that she had located another book in which he might be interested. It was not a book on symbols, she warned. But the trip, she assured him, would be worth the effort.

And so there Julian stood—one last time—at the front of the store, as Ms. Craddock pulled a small brown book from beneath her counter and handed it to him.

"It was part of a large estate my late husband purchased many, many years ago," she explained. "A French family, I believe."

Julian looked at the book and gasped.

On the cover—directly beneath the book's title—was the Greek letter sigma—Σ.

He carefully opened the book.

On the frontispiece—the page opposite the title page—was an engraving of a hawk holding a spear.

He thumbed quickly through the rest of the book until he reached the last page. There, at the bottom of the page and following the last line of the text, was the printer's mark—the stamp used to identify the book's publisher. Julian recognized it instantly: a crescent moon over crossed quills. It was the Letterford family crest.

CHAPTER SIX
Luggage

Luggage—Containers for a traveler's belongings.

Manchester, Georgia
Saturday, June 2

The letter sat on the far corner of her desk. It was postmarked Abergavenny, Wales. Colophon hadn't thought about it for months. But today she slipped the handwritten letter out of the envelope.

> Colophon:
> There is no time for small talk.
> In our quest, we followed one clue to
> another, which led us to the Shake-
> speare manuscripts. We all assumed

*the manuscripts were, in fact, Miles
Letterford's great treasure.
We were wrong.
The manuscripts were simply
another clue.
I will write further.
Julian*

The words now jumped off the page: *The manuscripts were simply another clue.*

Her brother was right. They needed help. They needed Julian.

It wasn't that she was opposed to asking Julian to help. Asking was easy. Julian was a great guy—and very smart. He would help in any way he could. The problem was that she was scheduled to spend the next four weeks at the dreadful camp in the middle of the woods in North Carolina. And she didn't have four weeks to waste.

There was only one thing to do.

Tell the truth.

She found her mother sitting at the kitchen table reading the newspaper and sipping coffee.

"Mom?" Colophon asked.

Meg Letterford looked up from the paper. "Yes, dear?"

Colophon braced herself. "I . . . don't want to go to camp this summer."

She was prepared for the inevitable. She knew how much the camp meant to her father. She knew that her parents had already paid for her stay at the camp and that it was probably too late to receive a refund. She knew that there were lots of reasons —good reasons—that she should go. And she knew that her mother would calmly explain all of those reasons to her.

But she didn't.

"You don't have to go to camp this summer if you don't want to," her mother said.

Colophon was stunned. "What?"

Meg motioned for her to sit down at the table. "I know you don't want to go to camp. And you don't have to go."

"But what about Dad? Won't he be disappointed?"

"It was his idea," her mother replied. "He knows you don't love camp the way we did. And he understands that this has been a rough week for everybody."

Colophon nodded.

Meg put the newspaper down on the table and took off her reading glasses. "There's more, isn't there?"

"Yes," Colophon said. "I need to go to London."

"London?"

"I have to see Julian."

Meg took a long sip from her coffee. "You're up to something, aren't you?" she finally replied.

Colophon didn't know what to say. A million thoughts raced through her mind.

Fortunately, Meg spared her daughter any further worry. "Your father is returning to London soon. I wasn't planning on going with him, but if you're going, I will too. I don't think he'll mind a little company on the trip."

"Great!" Colophon exclaimed. "But what about Case? If he goes with us, he'll miss summer baseball."

"Case can stay with the Parker family until baseball is over. I can't ask him to miss the rest of the season. And besides, his teammates are counting on him."

Colophon noticed that her mother did not seem particularly happy about leaving her older child with another family while they jetted off across the ocean. "I don't like splitting us up like this," Meg added.

Colophon grabbed her mother's hand and squeezed it tight. "We'll all be together soon," she said. "And everything will be okay. Just wait and see."

✦ ✦ ✦

The Waterside Inn
Cardiff, Wales
Sunday, June 3, 10:32 a.m.

Julian stared down at the text from Colophon. She was going to be in London on Tuesday. She needed to meet with him immediately. She said it was urgent.

He checked the train schedules on his laptop. It was a two-and-a-half-hour ride from Cardiff to Charing Cross Station in London. He purchased a ticket for Tuesday morning.

He texted her back: "Arriving Tuesday around lunch. See you then."

Julian sat back in his chair. Several newspapers were scattered across his bed. For most of the prior week he had been out of touch with the rest of the world. He had a tendency to do that—to hole up in some remote location and pore over old books and manuscripts for days on end. Cell phones, computers, the Internet, television, and newspapers were distractions—and he simply ignored them. He had just learned this morning about the controversy over the Shakespeare manuscripts when he glimpsed the name "Letterford" on the front page of a newspaper in the café down the street. And that made his discovery in Hay-on-Wye—that dusty old long-forgotten book—even more troubling.

Sir Hedley Penrose shuffled into the front parlor of his house. The years had not been kind to him. What hair remained on his head seemed to grow directly from his ears. His thick, cloudy glasses hung far down on the end of his large nose. He was a heavy man with thick jowls and deep bags under his eyes. Every step he took seemed to require great effort.

"Mr. Treemont?" His voice was stern. Clearly he was not pleased at dealing with an unexpected visitor—particularly this visitor.

Treemont extended his right hand. "A pleasure."

Sir Penrose ignored Treemont's hand and gestured toward a chair by the fireplace. "Sit," he instructed.

Although it was almost seventy-five degrees outside, a fire roared in the fireplace. Treemont settled into one of the large cane chairs near the hearth. "I want to thank you for taking the time to meet with me on such short notice."

Penrose grunted. "I can't say that I'm particularly pleased." He grabbed a poker and stirred the fire. Sparks shot into the room.

"I presume you wish to discuss the manuscripts?" he finally said. The question carried a heavy tone of disapproval.

Treemont knew that Sir Penrose prided himself on his independence and objectivity. He would meet any efforts to influence the outcome of his investigation with fierce opposition. Treemont was counting on that.

"No," replied Treemont.

The answer caught Sir Penrose off guard. "Excuse me?"

"It would not be appropriate to discuss the manuscripts," said Treemont.

"Hear, hear," said Sir Penrose. "So then, if I may ask — what exactly is the purpose of your visit?"

"As you may be aware, I have been asked to monitor the operations of Letterford and Sons — on a temporary basis, of course."

Sir Penrose nodded. He was well aware of the situation at the publishing house.

Treemont continued. "As you may imagine, there

are certain people within the organization who want nothing more than a quick resolution to this issue."

Sir Penrose was immediately suspicious. "And you do not?"

"No," replied Treemont. "I want a proper resolution, no matter how long it takes."

Sir Penrose sat back in his chair. "And may I ask why?"

Treemont paused briefly for effect and stared at the fire. Trigue James had told him to take it slow —to be patient. *Don't let it appear rehearsed.* After a moment, he turned back to Sir Penrose. "Sir, the reputation of Letterford and Sons is on the line—a reputation built over four centuries."

"A sterling reputation," Sir Penrose agreed. "But I cannot be asked to protect it."

"Nor should you," replied Treemont. "A reputation built on centuries of hard work and a commitment to excellence should not rise or fall on the authenticity of these . . . so-called Shakespeare manuscripts."

Treemont let his statement float around the room for a brief moment.

"The manuscripts," he continued, "are either real or they are not. If they are real, history will not care if it took three, five, or even ten years to make that determination. If they are not real, however, history will thank those responsible for taking the time to do it right. Letterford and Sons should stand unquestionably in support of a thorough and complete examination—nothing less. History will judge our company by our commitment to the truth."

"Quite right!" exclaimed Sir Penrose. "As a matter of fact, I said almost the exact same thing in—"

"—your report on the West Upton Sewer situation."

"You're familiar with my report?" asked Sir Penrose. There was excitement in his voice.

"Chapter and verse," Treemont replied.

Sir Penrose stirred the fire. Sparks once again shot into the room. Treemont sat back and waited. Sir Penrose set the poker down and leaned forward in his chair. "I can assure you that this report will be handled with every bit of the care and dedication that were put into the West Upton report. I shall take every minute, every day, every year necessary to get it right! No one shall influence me to rush to a quick decision."

Treemont nodded solemnly. "For history."

"Aye," replied Sir Penrose. "For history."

CHAPTER SEVEN
Fitful

Fitful—Occurring in or characterized by
intermittent bursts, as of activity; irregular.

Letterford Residence
Clerkenwell, London, England
Tuesday, June 5
12:15 p.m.

Colophon paced up and down the entrance hall, stopping occasionally to peer out the front door at the street below. She saw lots of cars, taxis, and pedestrians—but no Julian.

She looked down at her watch.

Where is he?

She took a deep breath. Getting worked up would not get him here any faster. She needed to stay calm.

After five more minutes, she stopped pacing, pulled out her cell phone, and punched in Julian's number.

He answered immediately. "Hello?"

"Where are you?" she demanded.

"Standing right outside your front door."

She turned around and there he was—tall, skinny, and scraggly as ever—waving at her from the window next to the front door. It had been several months since she had last seen him. She knew people changed over time, and that worried her. Would he be different? Would he still be willing to listen to her—to take her seriously? But one look at the eyes peering down at her over his slightly askew glasses told her everything she needed to know—Julian was still Julian. She rushed to the door and opened it.

"C'mon," she said as she turned and headed toward the library.

Julian dropped his bag in the foyer. "Wait a second. No hug for your favorite cousin?"

She stopped. "Sorry." She gave him a quick hug. "I'm just a little anxious."

He stooped over, pulled a small package from his bag, and slipped it into the front pocket of his jacket. "I know. We have a lot to talk about."

"You don't know the half of it," replied Colophon.

Letterford Library
Clerkenwell, London, England
Tuesday, June 5
12:35 p.m.

Colophon placed the inkwell under the lamp on the reading table.

"There," she said.

Julian stared at it. "There what?"

"There on the cap—can't you see it?"

He bent over until his face was just inches from the inkwell's cap. "There seem to be some scratches on it. And it's shiny."

"Scratches? Honestly, your eyes are terrible." She flipped open her laptop. A moment later she turned the screen around to show him. "I took a picture of it. Here's an enlargement."

"Wow!" exclaimed Julian. "It's some sort of crest and a Latin inscription—'Qvod me nvtrit me destrvit.'"

"It means 'That which nourishes me destroys me.'"
Colophon felt pleased to be able to give the translation to Julian.

"Nice translation—and very cryptic," he said. "But
why did I have to come all the way to London to see
this? Couldn't you have e-mailed it?"

"Because we have to prove the manuscripts are
real," said Colophon. "And this is our first clue. My
dad said this inkwell might've belonged to Shakespeare. Maybe it'll help us prove that he really wrote
the manuscripts."

"Hold on," replied Julian. "Didn't I read in the paper that some sort of group is being set up to study
the manuscripts?"

"Yes, a special commission, but it's going to take
them *years*. My dad can't wait that long."

"Why not?"

"The family has asked Treemont to oversee the
company!" she replied.

Julian sank back in his chair. "I didn't know that."

"Treemont will do anything he can to get the family business," she said. "And the longer it takes to
study the manuscripts . . ."

"The better for Treemont," said Julian.

"Exactly."

"Have you told your father about the inscription on the inkwell?" asked Julian.

She shook her head. "No. He'd want me to turn it over to the commission to study. He would never allow me—us—to do anything that might interfere with the commission. But I can't sit back and hope they figure this out."

"But they're experts," he said.

"We discovered the manuscripts," replied Colophon. "We have to do this."

Julian stood up, walked over to the window, and peered down at the street below. He could feel the weight of the small package in his jacket pocket. He decided it was best to let it sit there a while longer.

Chapter Eight
Instinctively

Instinctively —Arising from impulse or
natural inclination; done without thought
or conscious effort; spontaneous.

Letterford Library
Clerkenwell, London, England
Tuesday, June 5
12:55 p.m.

Julian slid the drawing across the table to Colophon.

"Not bad," she said.

"Are you kidding?" he retorted. "It's a perfect copy

of the crest on the inkwell—and a lot clearer than the photos you tried to take."

She rolled her eyes. "Okay, fine—it's perfect—but we still haven't figured out what it means."

She placed the drawing in the middle of the table.

The image appeared to be a crest or a coat of arms —that much seemed clear. It was in the shape of a shield divided into four quadrants. There were two basic symbols on the shield: a bird and flowers. The problem was that they didn't know what kind of bird or what kind of flowers.

"This could take a few weeks," Julian warned. "We need to get a copy of *Pimbley's Dictionary of Heraldry,* and there are several registries for ancient coats of arms. We may have to look at hundreds— maybe thousands—of them to narrow this down. If that doesn't work, we can begin to break down the individual symbols. What traits do these symbols represent? Is there a particular combination of bird and flower that has special significance?"

"Or," said Colophon, "we can Google it."

"Okay," said Julian. "Let's see how that works out."

She Googled the terms *bird flowers coat of arms.*

The search came back with about 3,940,000 results.

"Well, that should narrow it down a bit," he said.

She ignored him.

She tried the terms *bird flowers coat of arms Shakespeare.*

That search came back with about 25,800,000 results.

"I know real research is boring and lacks instant gratification," said Julian, "but it might be called for in this particular instance. This isn't going to just fall in our laps."

Colophon sighed. "Maybe you're right."

"I'm sorry," he said. "I must be getting hard of hearing—could you repeat that?"

"I said maybe you're right—this time."

He grinned. "Thank you."

A knock on the library door interrupted their discussion. Meg Letterford walked in carrying a tray of sandwiches and drinks. "Can I offer anyone some lunch?"

"That would be great," said Julian.

"Thanks, Mom," added Colophon.

Meg placed the tray on the table. "Dare I ask what you're doing?"

Julian and Colophon looked at each other.

"Well," Colophon said, "it's complicated."

Meg looked at her daughter. "As long as 'compli-

cated' doesn't lead to another dangerous underground crypt, then I'm okay with it." She shot a look
at Julian. "Understood?"

"Yes, ma'am," he and Colophon replied in unison.

"Fine," said Meg. "Then I'll leave you to your work."

She stepped outside the library and started to pull
the door shut. "Oh, one last thing," she said.

Colophon and Julian looked up from their food.

Meg pointed at Julian's drawing in the middle of
the table. "I've spent my fair share of time at Cambridge University, and I'm certain that's the crest of
Corpus Christi College."

Letterford Library
Clerkenwell, London, England
Tuesday, June 5
1:25 p.m.

Julian and Colophon stared at the computer screen.
A couple of half-eaten sandwiches sat forgotten on
the table.

There it was.

A little clearer and crisper, and in bright colors.
Meg Letterford was right. It was exactly the same as
the engraving on the top of the inkwell—the crest
for Corpus Christi College at Cambridge University.

The birds on the crest, they learned, were pelicans, and the flowers were lilies. Julian explained that the pelican was a medieval symbol of self-sacrifice, while the lilies signified purity.

"I've heard of Cambridge University," said Colophon. "But what's Corpus Christi College?"

"Cambridge University is made up of a bunch of different colleges," replied Julian. "But the colleges are not the same as they are in the United States. The students from all the different colleges at Cambridge attend classes together, but their college is where they live, eat, and socialize. They may graduate from Cambridge University, but they will forever identify themselves with the college where they lived."

"Sort of like Hogwarts?" asked Colophon. "Once a Gryffindor, always a Gryffindor?"

Julian paused. "Sort of. But each college has its own building and grounds. Corpus Christi is one of the smallest, but it's very beautiful."

"Was Corpus Christi College around when Miles Letterford was alive?"

He chuckled. "Cambridge University is almost eight hundred years old. And Corpus Christi is getting close to seven hundred years old."

"Then we need to go to Cambridge," said Colophon.

"It's not very far from London, right? The next clue could be there."

Julian stood up and walked over to the fireplace. "But what if there's not another clue? The inkwell could be just that—a bottle with an inscription—nothing more. Simply a memento from Cambridge. A souvenir, perhaps. A golden key doesn't pop out of everything." He looked up at the tellurian.

The question caught Colophon off guard. It was the type of thing her father would say, not Julian. She sat back in her seat and cradled the inkwell in her hands.

"Can I ask you a question?" she finally said. "Did you ever doubt that Miles Letterford had put a clue to the family treasure in his portrait?"

Julian paused for a moment. "No."

"Even though half the family thought you were crazy, you believed."

"Yes, I believed."

"And I believed in you," she said.

He paused again, staring at the silver orb attached to the brass rod on the tellurian. In that same silver orb a golden key had improbably been found, just a few months ago.

"And I believe in you," he said. "So I guess we need to go to Cambridge."

She smiled.

"Well," he continued, "now we just have to find a way to get into Corpus Christi College and search the grounds for some sort of clue—even though we have no idea what that clue might be or where it might be hidden. That certainly sounds easy enough."

She slumped back in her chair. "Good point. How do we get into the college?"

"Study hard."

"Very funny," she replied. "I'm serious."

"I know you're serious," he said. "But we can't just waltz in there and start snooping about the place."

He was right—they couldn't simply walk into the college and roam the grounds. But there must be a way. Colophon looked down at the drawing of the crest for Corpus Christi College. Julian had said the pelican was a symbol of self-sacrifice.

"I know how we can search the college," she finally said.

CHAPTER NINE
Accused

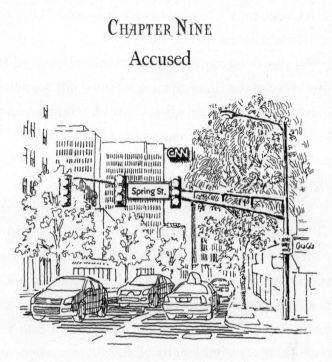

Accused—Charged with a shortcoming or error.

Marietta Street
Atlanta, Georgia
Monday, June 11
8:35 a.m.

The weather had been unseasonably cool—and for Georgia in June, that was a good thing. With the temperature hovering around seventy-five degrees and the skies cloudy, Mull had decided to walk the five blocks from his downtown office to CNN Center.

He needed the break.

All the news outlets that had once celebrated the discovery of the Shakespeare manuscripts were now questioning whether they were forgeries—solely based on the word of one man. A man, it might be added, who had seemingly disappeared from the face of the earth since his pronouncement.

The press was having a field day with the story. That a commission had been set up in England to study the manuscripts seemed only to confirm their suspicions. Mull, however, was not concerned about the results of the commission's inquiry—the documents were real, he knew. What troubled him was both the excessive length of the investigation and the public mistrust about the manuscripts and the family business.

The rumbling among family members also weighed upon him. Once again, they had called into question his leadership of the company. But this time the issue was more than his leadership. Certain members of the family—members who knew the manuscripts were real—had aligned themselves with Treemont. What puzzled and anguished him was: why?

Clearly Mull needed to take some sort of action to calm the situation. Several prominent document examiners and academics had already attested to the manuscripts' authenticity, both before and after Reginald Whitmore's press conference. Their conclusions needed to be brought out publicly. The reputation of Letterford & Sons had to be defended. And so Mull had agreed to an interview on CNN. The producer had promised him a fair opportunity to present his side of the controversy, but had also warned that tough questions would be asked. Mull was ready to answer those questions.

Marietta Street
Atlanta, Georgia
Monday, June 11
8:35 a.m.

Following someone through the streets of a busy city without being noticed is easy. The true test of skill, however, is to remain ahead of your target, not behind him. But Trigue James was skilled. He would allow Mull Letterford to close the distance between them at just the right time.

✳ ✳ ✳

Corner of Spring and Marietta Streets
Atlanta, Georgia
Monday, June 11
8:45 a.m.

Mull stood in a small crowd waiting for the light to change. He could see the entrance to CNN Center a block ahead to his left. He took a deep breath. The interview was set to take place at 9:30 a.m. He reminded himself to stay calm and focus on the facts.

Corner of Spring and Marietta Streets
Atlanta, Georgia
Monday, June 11
8:45 a.m.

Three people now stood between Mull Letterford and Trigue James. James could see Letterford behind him in the windows of the cars passing through the intersection. Timing would be critical. James gripped his cane tightly.

CHAPTER TEN
Amazement

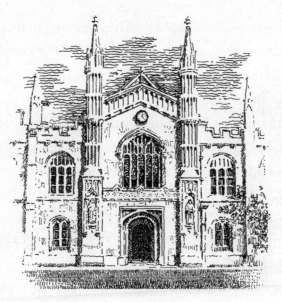

Amazement—A state of extreme
surprise or wonder; astonishment.

Corpus Christi College
Cambridge, England
Monday, June 11
12:45 p.m.

The taxi dropped off Colophon and Julian just outside the college's main gate.

"I still don't know how you plan on getting about the college," Julian said as they walked toward the entrance. "And why all the secrecy for the last few days?"

"Trust me," she replied. "They're going to let us see whatever we want." And with that, she brushed past him and entered the porter's lodge inside the main gate.

Julian paused momentarily and stared at the open door to the porter's lodge. Three days ago Colophon had announced that they needed to be at Corpus Christi College on the following Monday. Despite his best efforts, she had refused to discuss the matter any further. "Monday," she had said. "You'll find out on Monday."

She stuck her head outside the door. "Are you coming?" she asked impatiently.

Julian nodded and followed her into the office.

A proper-looking older gentleman stood behind the counter. On his dark blue blazer was the crest for the college—the same pelicans and lilies that Colophon had found on the cap of the inkwell. Several other gentlemen—all similarly dressed—milled around the office.

"May I help you?" the gentleman asked politely.

"Yes, my name is Colophon Letterford, and I believe Ms. Cadewaller is expecting me."

The gentleman smiled. "She is indeed expecting you. I'm Ashby Scolfield, the head porter. I'm afraid that Ms. Cadewaller is running a bit late. She asked me to extend her apologies and offer you a cup of tea or, if you prefer, hot chocolate, while you wait."

"A cup of hot chocolate would be great," she said.

"Excellent choice," the porter replied. "The dining hall makes a magnificent hot chocolate—the key is the steamed milk." He motioned toward a door on the far side of the office. "If you will please follow me. Ms. Cadewaller asked that you wait for her in the fellows' combination room."

They followed Scolfield out of the lodge and into a large square courtyard within the college. In the center of the courtyard was a huge, immaculately maintained grass lawn. Small brass signs around the perimeter reminded the forgetful to stay off the grass. A broad stone walkway surrounded the lawn, and in turn, the courtyard was enclosed on all four sides by massive stone buildings that belonged in some fairy tale. At the far side of the courtyard was a tall building with two spires that towered high above the surrounding structures. A large stained-glass window looked down over the courtyard, and above the stained glass was a large clock with gold hands and a deep red face.

Colophon stood on the pathway and took it all in. "Wow."

"First time to Corpus?" asked the porter.

"Yes, sir."

"I came here forty-five years ago from a small village in Ireland," Scolfield said. "I can still remember the first time I stepped into this very courtyard." He paused and looked down at her. "I know how you feel. It can be a bit overwhelming."

She nodded. It did seem overwhelming. How would they ever find the next clue? It seemed an impossible task.

"As odd as it may sound," the porter continued, "this is actually New Court. The large building with the clock tower is the chapel. The building to the right of the clock tower is the Parker Library. And over to the left—where we are headed—are the dining hall and combination room."

"New Court?" said Colophon. "This place looks like it's been around forever."

"True," the porter replied. "But relatively speaking, it's a modern addition to Corpus." He motioned for them to follow him along the stone path, which took them around the corner to a small passageway. The passageway led to a smaller—but no less impressive—courtyard.

"This, on the other hand," he said, "is Old Court."

"How old?" she asked.

"Well, the exact date is not known, but it's believed that construction was completed sometime around 1352. What you see here today is basically the exact same scene that would have greeted a Cambridge student six hundred years ago."

"Wow," Colophon said again.

Scolfield opened the door at the corner of the courtyard. "This way."

Julian and Colophon stepped into a large wood-paneled hall with a high ceiling painted in gold, red, and black. Three rows of long tables with white linens, table settings, and straight-back wooden chairs ran the length of the hall. Large, ornate chandeliers hung from the ceiling, and huge ancient portraits crowded the walls.

"This is the dining hall," the porter said as they walked. "Members of the college and the fellows take their meals in here—breakfast, lunch, and dinner."

They continued to the far end of the room—to a raised platform and yet another long table. It too was set with white linens and surrounded by wooden chairs.

"Who sits up here?" asked Colophon. "It looks important." It all seemed so Harry Potterish to her.

"This table is reserved for the fellows of the college," replied the porter.

"What's a fellow?" asked Colophon.

"My sincerest apologies," he said. "A fellow is a teacher. I should have taken the time to explain that."

Scolfield opened a door behind the fellows' table and escorted Julian and Colophon into an ornately decorated room. On the far side was a large fireplace. A small portrait hung over the mantel. A window on either side looked down over New Court. Large portraits with thick gilded frames hung on every wall, and in the middle of the room stood a couch and several chairs. Empty teacups and newspapers were scattered on small tables throughout.

"This is the fellows' combination room," Scolfield said. He looked at Colophon. "You'll have to excuse the mess—it's sort of a gathering place for the fellows."

He once again extended his hand to her. "It has been a pleasure meeting you, young Ms. Letterford. I'll have someone from the kitchen bring around some tea and hot chocolate in short order. I do hope you have a pleasant visit to Corpus."

And with that Ashby Scolfield excused himself.

"Okay," said Julian, "who is Ms. Cadewaller, and how did you get us in here?"

"Ms. Cadewaller works for the college's library. I asked if she would provide a tour in exchange for an . . . opportunity for the college."

"An opportunity?"

Colophon opened her backpack and pulled out a small object that she placed on a tea table. It was the inkwell.

"You didn't!" he exclaimed. "You can't give that away!"

"I didn't give it away," she replied. "I would never do that. I simply told Ms. Cadewaller about the inkwell and asked if the college could help authenticate it. She jumped at the chance to see it. They're going to take some photographs of it while we tour the college."

Julian looked down at her. "Clever. So what's next?"

"We start where we can," she replied. "In this room." She pointed at the portraits on the walls. "For example, who are the people in these paintings? Any of them could be the next clue. We need to find out who all these guys are and whether they had any connection to Shakespeare or Miles Letterford."

"That's a pretty tall order," he said. "What if we start by narrowing it down to portraits painted around the same time as the portrait of Miles—say, the early seventeenth century?"

Colophon agreed. After all, the portrait of Miles Letterford had provided their first clue.

Julian and Colophon examined a massive painting that hung near the entrance to the dining hall. According to the brass plate on the frame, the very large man it depicted was a former master of the college. The date of the portrait, however, was all wrong —it had been painted at least a hundred years after the portrait of Miles Letterford.

They looked at three more portraits in the room —but all failed to satisfy their basic criterion.

"Perhaps Ms. Cadewaller can provide a list of the portraits at the college and the dates they were painted," suggested Julian. "That might narrow it down."

Colophon nodded. His suggestion seemed reasonable—but there was so much ground to cover and so many potential clues, and they had not even started their tour. Still, there was one more portrait in the combination room, and since Ms. Cadewaller had yet to make her appearance, Colophon decided that there was no sense in wasting time. She gazed up at the portrait hanging high over the fireplace mantel. It seemed oddly out of place. It was small compared to the rest of the portraits in the room. It had a simple wooden frame. And the man in the portrait was young—very young.

A student perhaps?

The man in the painting lacked the stately bearing of the men in the other portraits. He had a thin mustache, and his brown hair was long and unkempt. He stood with his arms crossed—almost defiant. And on his face was the slightest hint of mischief, almost as if he was mocking the formality of the other paintings. He certainly didn't look like a fellow or a master of the college. And yet the portrait hung in such a prominent place.

Curious.

And then something else caught Colophon's attention. The young man wore a coat with large gold buttons that ran down his sleeves and up his chest. With his arms crossed, the buttons formed a symbol she had seen time and time again—a sigma. The symbol was turned sideways—but it was unmistakable.

Probably just a coincidence, she thought.

Still, a very curious coincidence.

Colophon walked over to the fireplace to get a better look. She noticed some writing in the painting's top-left corner, but the deep shadows from the frame made it difficult to read the words from below.

Colophon pointed to the portrait. "Can you read what it says?" she asked Julian.

He walked over to the fireplace. "No, it's too high on the wall—too many shadows."

Her eyes never left the painting. "I need to get closer."

Julian pulled over one of the chairs. "Quick," he said. "See what it says before they get here with the tea and hot chocolate."

She climbed up on the chair, stood on her tiptoes, and moved as close to the painting as she could. The light was dim, and she had to squint to read the words. Calmly, she climbed back down and stepped back off the chair.

"Well," he asked, "what did it say?"

"Do you think the hot chocolate will be here soon?" she asked nonchalantly.

"What did it say?"

She smiled. "See for yourself," she said.

He stood on the chair and looked at the top-left corner of the painting. Immediately to the left of the man's head were five words: QVOD ME NVTRIT ME DESTRVIT.

CHAPTER ELEVEN
Mimic

Mimic — One who copies or imitates closely,
especially in speech, expression, and gesture.

Corner of Spring and Marietta Streets
Atlanta, Georgia
Monday, June 11
8:46 a.m.

The light changed. Mull stepped off the curb and into
the intersection. The crowd streamed around an elderly man who was shuffling across the street with
a cane. The man and Mull reached the far side of
the intersection at the same moment. Just as Mull
stepped onto the curb, the elderly man tripped and
fell to the sidewalk. His cane dropped at Mull's feet.

Mull picked up the cane and reached down to help
the man. "Are you okay?"

The elderly man appeared embarrassed and barely made eye contact with Mull. "Guess I missed the curb," he muttered.

"Happens to everyone now and then," Mull replied.

"I suppose."

Mull looked at his watch. He had to get on over to the studio at CNN Center. "Do you need me to call an ambulance?"

"Heck no," the man replied. "If I can survive the Korean War and fifty years of marriage, I think I can survive a fall on the sidewalk."

Mull grinned and handed the man his cane. "I suppose you can. Take care of yourself."

"That I will," the elderly man replied. "And thanks for the help."

"All in a day's work," Mull said as he turned and walked toward CNN Center.

Corner of Spring and Marietta Streets
Atlanta, Georgia
Monday, June 11
8:48 a.m.

Trigue James stood and watched Mull Letterford walk away. James never ceased to be amazed at the ability of people to see what they expect to see rather than what is directly in front of them. To the casual observer, James looked like an old man. He shuffled when he walked. He was bent over. He wore a soft-brimmed fishing hat to shade his face. His hair and eyebrows were gray. Thick glasses covered his eyes. With a brown eyeliner, he had added just a few wrinkles around the corners of his mouth. But that was the extent of the disguise. Letterford had simply expected to see an old man, and that was what he had seen.

He never even noticed that James was wearing gloves.

James watched Letterford enter CNN Center. He then turned and walked two blocks back to a parking garage just off Marietta Street. It was an old, poorly maintained concrete mess that seemed on the verge of collapse. But it offered one particularly redeeming feature—it had no security cameras. James took the stairs up to the third level. He had parked his car in a corner, at a spot overlooking an alley.

Down below in the alley was an open trash bin. James had a clear view of it. No one was there. He looked around the parking deck, then used a disposable wipe to clean off his face. He ran a brush through his hair to remove the traces of gray. He dropped the wipe, the hat, the glasses, the wig, the cane, and the gloves into the open bin below. He knew that the solution on the cane would lose its potency within half an hour. Even if someone found the cane, the solution wouldn't be strong enough to kill.

Within ten minutes James was headed for the Atlanta airport.

CHAPTER TWELVE
Gossip

Gossip—To engage in or spread rumor or talk of a personal or sensational nature.

Fellows' Combination Room
Corpus Christi College
Cambridge, England
Monday, June 11
2:00 p.m.

Julian stepped off the chair and away from the fireplace just as the tea and hot chocolate were delivered.

The server placed the tray on a butler table near a small group of chairs and exited without a word.

Colophon took her hot chocolate and sat in a chair facing the fireplace. "Who do you think he is?" she asked as she slurped the mound of whipped cream off the top of the cup.

Julian sat down next to her and took a sip of tea. "I don't know. But don't get too excited. It could be just a coincidence—some sort of motto for the college. I told you, the inkwell might be just a souvenir. Maybe that phrase is on a lot of the paintings around this place. You know we've only seen one room."

She smiled. "Did you notice the shape of the buttons?"

"The buttons?" He turned in his seat and stared up at the painting. After a moment, he slowly turned his head sideways. He then straightened back up and took a sip of tea.

"Well?" she asked.

He looked down at his tea. "It steeped a bit long" —he paused—"and it needs more milk."

"The buttons! I'm talking about the buttons!"

"Oh," he said nonchalantly. "It's not a coincidence. That's clearly a sigma."

"Yes!" she said. "We found it—the clue! I just knew it!"

"A clue to what?" The voice came from the door at the back of the room. Colophon and Julian turned in their seats. In the doorway stood a tall, attractive woman. She wore a blue suit, and her dark brown hair was pulled back tightly into a bun.

The two visitors jumped up out of their seats. "Ms. Cadewaller?" said Colophon.

"Yes," said the woman as she strode across the room. "And I presume you are Ms. Letterford?"

"Yes." Colophon nodded. "And this is my cousin Julian."

"A pleasure," Doris Cadewaller said. "Now, you were saying something about a clue?"

"Oh," said Colophon, "we were discussing the portrait over the fireplace. Neither of us has a clue as to who it is."

"Ah, you have a good eye for a mystery."

Colophon and Julian looked at each other and then back at Ms. Cadewaller.

"What do you mean?" asked Julian.

Ms. Cadewaller walked over to the wall and flipped a switch. A small light over the portrait flickered and illuminated the entire painting.

Suddenly the colors seemed much richer than they had appeared earlier. And something seemed almost . . . familiar about the painting to Colophon.

"That," Ms. Cadewaller said, "is believed to be the only known portrait of Christopher Marlowe."

"Marlowe!" Julian exclaimed.

Colophon shot him a look.

"Who's Marlowe?" she asked.

"Next to William Shakespeare," Ms. Cadewaller responded, "Marlowe is perhaps the most important playwright and poet of the sixteenth century. And, I might add, he was a graduate of this college."

"You said something about a mystery," Julian interrupted. "What did you mean?"

"Well," she replied, "no one can say with absolute certainty that this is a portrait of Marlowe. The painting was found in 1952 under a fireplace in one of the resident rooms in Old Court."

"Under a fireplace?" said Colophon. "That seems odd."

"Odd indeed," the woman replied. "And it just so happens that the room in which it was found was directly above the room in which it is believed that Marlowe lodged at Corpus."

"But that could be a coincidence," said Julian. "Why do they think it's Marlowe?"

Ms. Cadewaller pointed at the top-left corner of the painting. "The inscription says the sitter was twenty-one years old in 1585. According to the college's records, Marlowe was the only student in 1585 who was twenty-one years old."

"Is that it?" asked Colophon. "Is there any other reason?"

"Absolutely," said Ms. Cadewaller. "Look at the other portraits in this room. And did you notice the portraits in the dining hall? Very distinguished-looking gentlemen, wouldn't you agree?"

"Yes," replied Colophon. *And a bit stodgy as well.*

"They all seem very proper, yes?"

Colophon nodded.

Ms. Cadewaller motioned toward the portrait above the fireplace. "And what about our young gentleman over the mantel?"

Colophon stared at the painting. "He looks like he's up to something."

Ms. Cadewaller laughed. "A wonderful description. And that, my dear, is another clue. Marlowe was cocky, brash, and bold—just like the man in the portrait. It seems to fit everything we know about Marlowe—that he attended Corpus, his age when he graduated, and quite frankly his attitude."

"What happened to Marlowe?" Colophon asked.

Doris Cadewaller paused, then said, "He died far too young. A pity. If he had lived, the world might have known as much about him as Shakespeare."

Colophon started to ask how he had died, but Julian interrupted her thought. "Any chance you could show us where Marlowe lodged while at the college?"

"Absolutely," Ms. Cadewaller replied cheerily. "And there are so many other wonderful things to show you as well." She motioned toward the inkwell on the tea table. "And is this the inkwell?" Excitement was evident in her voice.

"Yes," Colophon replied. "Please take good care of it. It means a lot to me."

"Rest assured," Ms. Cadewaller said, "it will be safe. We take great pride at Corpus in our preservation of history." She carefully wrapped the inkwell in newspaper and placed it in a small box. "Now a quick trip to my office to drop this off to be photographed, and then on with our tour."

Colophon remained standing in front of the fireplace. "Ms. Cadewaller?"

"Yes, dear?"

"Who painted the portrait of Marlowe?"

"Good question," the woman replied. "Unfortunately, no one knows. It's not signed." She turned and opened the door. "However," she said offhandedly, "the style is reminiscent of a relatively obscure portraitist."

"Oh?" asked Julian. "Who?"

"Dimplert Steumacher," she replied as she headed out the door to the courtyard.

Colophon and Julian stopped in their tracks.

"Steumacher!" Colophon whispered. The same man who had painted Miles Letterford's portrait!

Julian glanced over his shoulder at the portrait of the young man, then turned and followed Ms. Cadewaller into the courtyard.

His reaction surprised Colophon. She had expected him to be much more excited.

Chapter Thirteen
Puke

Puke—The act of vomiting.

Studio 6, CNN Center
Atlanta, Georgia
Monday, June 11
9:27 a.m.

It started with a twinge in his stomach.

Nerves, Mull told himself. *Nothing more.*

"Two minutes to air," someone yelled from behind the camera.

Mull took a sip of water as a technician adjusted the microphone on his tie.

The twinge grew worse. And he was growing hotter by the minute.

Must be the studio lights, Mull assured himself.

"One minute to air!" the voice yelled.

Richard Brayson, the host of CNN's *Newsmakers* program, asked Mull if he was ready. Mull nodded and gave a thumbs-up.

Mull took another sip of water, but his mouth was now dry as sand. His stomach was churning. The heat from the studio lights seemed to increase by the second.

"Thirty seconds!" the voice yelled.

Mull tried to focus on Brayson, but he was now seeing three of everything.

Was it food poisoning? What had he eaten for breakfast? He couldn't remember. Everything suddenly seemed foggy and distant.

"Ten!" the voice yelled.

He could feel the sweat beading on his forehead.

"Nine!"

His tongue felt as if it had swelled to twice its normal size.

"Eight! Seven! Six! Five!"

His left hand started to shake.

"Four!"

He could feel his heart rate increasing.

"Three! Two! One!" The director pointed at the host of the program.

"Good morning and welcome to CNN's *Newsmakers*," said Richard Brayson to the camera. "Earlier this year the discovery of the Shakespeare manuscripts was hailed as one of the greatest finds of the century. However, questions have now been raised about the authenticity of those documents. Are they real or an elaborate forgery? I am joined this morning by Mull Letterford, the president and owner of Letterford and Sons. Mr. Letterford has agreed to speak with me today about the Shakespeare manuscripts and the growing controversy over their authenticity."

Brayson swiveled in his seat and faced Mull. What he saw alarmed him. Mull was red-faced and sweating, and his left hand was visibly twitching. But Brayson was a professional. He had seen guests with severe stage fright. They usually got over it after a question or two. He decided to press forward. "Welcome, Mr. Letterford, and thank you for joining us this morning."

"Thank you for having me," Mull squeaked. Sweat beads covered his forehead. He took another sip of water.

"As you well know," Brayson continued, "questions have now been raised about the authenticity of the . . . Whitmore . . . the . . . portion . . . ink . . . paper . . ."

Mull stared at Brayson as he spoke, but the words didn't register. His head spun. He tried to focus on what the man was saying.

" . . . after . . . seven . . . mixed . . . opinion . . . and . . . possible forgery . . ."

The words tumbled in and around Mull without meaning.

" . . . conclude . . . appointed . . . top . . . commission . . ."

Mull leaned forward in his chair.

" . . . respond to Dr. Whitmore's claims?"

Mull could tell that Brayson had stopped speaking and now expected him to answer the question. The problem was that Mull had no idea what the question was.

He wiped his forehead with his sleeve and took another sip of water. "Would you mind repeating the question?" His voice was barely a whisper.

Richard Brayson looked at his director and mouthed the word *commercial*. The director nodded.

The camera panned to Brayson and, mercifully, away from Mull. "We'll be back after a brief commercial break," he said.

"We're out!" someone yelled.

Brayson removed his microphone and leaned over to Mull. "Are you okay?"

"No," Mull managed to say just before throwing up on Brayson's shoes.

Christopher Marlowe
1581-1587
John Fletcher
1591-1594
ANTIQVAE DOMVS
GEMINV MDECVS

Questioning — To ask a question
or questions of someone.

Corpus Christi College
Cambridge, England
Monday, June 11
2:30 p.m.

Julian, Colophon, and Doris Cadewaller stood in
front of a large brass plaque affixed to an exterior
wall facing into Old Court. It read:

Christopher Marlowe

1581–1587

John Fletcher

1591–1594

ANTIQVAE DOMVS

GEMINV MDECVS

Colophon pointed to the windows on either side of the plaque. "Was that Marlowe's room?"

"As best as we can determine," replied Ms. Cadewaller. "The portrait was found in the room just above it."

Colophon peered through the window located on the right side of the plaque. A young woman sitting at a desk stared back at her. Colophon jumped.

"There's someone in there!" she said.

"Why, yes," replied Ms. Cadewaller. "Our students still reside in these rooms. This is a college, you know."

Colophon did know that it was a college, but she remained amazed that students still lived in rooms that were hundreds of years old—and formerly occupied by famous playwrights.

She pointed to the plaque. "It took Marlowe seven years to graduate?"

"Yes," Ms. Cadewaller replied. She paused momentarily. "He had certain . . . interruptions in his studies."

"And who was John Fletcher?" Colophon asked. "Why is he on the plaque?"

"Another famous alumnus of Corpus," she replied, "and like Marlowe, an outstanding playwright."

Colophon was puzzled. "How come I've never heard of him?"

"It's not surprising," replied her guide. "Shakespeare's shadow has eclipsed many of the famous playwrights of that era. It's a pity. Fletcher was a talented dramatist and collaborated with Shakespeare on several plays. Some historians have suggested that he may have been an apprentice of sorts to Shakespeare."

Marlowe, Fletcher, Shakespeare.

Everything, Colophon thought, always seemed to work its way back to Shakespeare.

Corpus Christi College
Cambridge, England
Monday, June 11
3:00 p.m.

The remainder of the tour of the college was a blur

for Colophon. She nodded at the appropriate points as Ms. Cadewaller discussed the unique architectural features of a particular building; she feigned amazement at stories of the college; and she asked a random question or two so as not to insult their host. But truth be told, she could have recited back little, if any, of what the tour guide had said over the last half hour or so. Colophon simply could not focus on anything but Christopher Marlowe and his connection to the inkwell.

She now found herself walking far behind Julian and Ms. Cadewaller as they headed through New Court and back to the entrance to the college to pick up the inkwell and depart. The tour was nearing its end, yet Colophon felt no closer to uncovering the next clue—if there was, in fact, a next clue to be found.

Exactly what was the connection that had brought them to this wonderful old college? she wondered.

Was the inkwell merely a memento of a friend— a colleague—treasured by Shakespeare? Or, as she desperately hoped, was it yet another clue left by Miles Letterford that could help prove Shakespeare authored the manuscripts?

It all seemed so confusing and so much out of her control.

She stopped suddenly.

But it's not out of my control, she realized.

It occurred to Colophon that she had simply left too much to chance. The inkwell had led them to Corpus Christi College, but they had simply stumbled on the Marlowe portrait.

It had been pure luck — nothing more.

There was no more time for luck. A question needed to be asked, and she needed to ask it.

"Ms. Cadewaller?"

Julian and Doris Cadewaller stopped just short of the entrance and turned around to face her.

"Yes?" the tour guide responded.

"Other than the portrait of Marlowe and his room, is there anything else that Marlowe might have left here at the college? Maybe a book or something?"

Ms. Cadewaller thought for a moment, then replied, "Not that I am aware of. And I'm fairly certain that I would know."

Colophon was disappointed. Once again they were in the right place but had no idea what the clue meant or even if it was the right clue.

"Of course," Ms. Cadewaller said, "there is the Matriculation Quill."

"The what?"

"The Matriculation Quill. Each year the new students — freshers, we call them — attend a ceremony where they sign a form that officially commences their studies at Cambridge. For centuries the new students signed their forms using a silver quill—the Matriculation Quill. A ballpoint pen is used today, but the quill remains one of the college's most treasured possessions."

"But what does it have to do with Marlowe?" Julian asked. "Was it his quill?"

"No," replied Ms. Cadewaller. "The quill was given to the college by an anonymous donor in 1621 in honor of Christopher Marlowe."

"And no one knows who donated it?" asked Colophon.

"Not a soul. It was delivered in an engraved silver box—the same box in which it is kept to this day. No name was attached, and no one has ever claimed credit."

"Was there anything on the box?" asked Colophon.

"A symbol perhaps?" asked Julian.

Colophon and Julian stared at Doris Cadewaller, who seemed taken back at the rush of questions and the sudden interest in the quill. "Why, yes," she stammered. "There are several odd symbols on the box, but the biggest is a large inscription on the top—"

Colophon knew what she was going to say before she said it.

"—a Greek letter. Sigma, I believe."

Bingo!

"Can we see the quill?" Colophon asked excitedly.

"I'm afraid that might be somewhat difficult to arrange," the tour guide replied. "The gentleman who is in charge of the college's silver collection, Norris Tanahill, is . . . shall we say, a bit of a curmudgeon."

"Can we at least ask?" said Colophon.

Doris Cadewaller paused and took a deep breath. "We can ask," she finally replied. "But I can't make any promises."

CHAPTER FIFTEEN

Gnarled

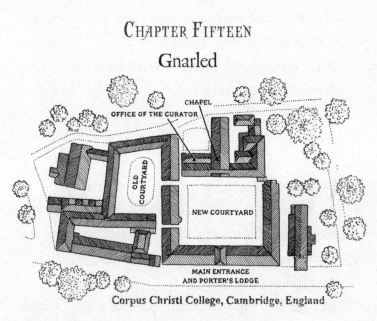

Corpus Christi College, Cambridge, England

Gnarled — Rugged and roughened,
as from old age or work.

Office of the Curator, Corpus Christi College
Cambridge, England
Monday, June 11
3:15 p.m.

The room was small, hot, and poorly lit. Dark wooden panels on the walls and ceiling gave it a gloomy, claustrophobic feel. A large wooden desk occupied most of the room. In front of the desk stood a short thin man with his arms crossed. He glared at Colophon and Julian from behind huge white, untamed, bushy eyebrows—the largest Colophon had ever seen. The tips of his ears were bright red.

"Nay," he said in a thick Scottish brogue.

"But—" Julian protested.

"Nay."

"Just a peek?"

"Nay."

"Perhaps—"

"Er' ye deaf? I said nay. Until ye have written permission from the master of the college, ye'll not see the quill. And that's final. No exceptions."

"And the master is—"

"In France," the man said. "And he won't be back for another week."

To be fair, they had been warned. Doris Cadewaller had told them that Norris Tanahill, the curator of the college's silver collection, was a curmudgeon of the worst sort. She had told them he could be rude, brusque, and, at times, downright belligerent. And she had been right—which probably explained why she had so unceremoniously left them as soon as she made the introductions.

Tanahill, as he made exceptionally clear, had no intention of allowing them to examine the Matriculation Quill, even though it lay in its box in a display case directly behind his desk. They could see it from across the room—but that was as close as Tanahill intended to allow them to get to it. And he seemed to be enjoying himself. He pointed at Julian. "For thirty years I have taken care of the college's silver. Thirty years! My job is to take care of the silver, not serve as a tour guide for a little girl and her babysitter."

Little girl! Babysitter!

Colophon seethed.

Norris Tanahill or not, she decided that she was going to get a close-up view of that silver quill.

But how?

She looked around. The room was windowless. A small coal-burning fireplace adorned the wall at one end of the room, and Tanahill's large oak desk sat at the other end, in front of the display case. The case did not appear to be locked. All she needed was a couple of minutes in the room by herself.

But again, how?

Then it hit her. Without drawing attention to herself, she reached inside her backpack and quietly took out her cell phone. A few moments later she was finished. She returned the phone to her backpack and set it against the wall near her feet.

"Again, nay, nay, nay," Tanahill said. "Ye'll not see the quill." The redness in his ears had spread to the rest of his face.

Julian started to press the issue once more when Colophon spoke up. "Thank you for your time, Mr. Tanahill. We'll be on our way now."

The pronouncement caught both Julian and Tanahill off guard.

"Pardon?" the curator asked.

Colophon looked at Julian, who was clearly puzzled. It was completely unlike her to give up so easily.

She looked Julian directly in the eyes. "It's time to go," she said slowly but emphatically.

It took a moment, but he finally realized—she had a plan.

"Ah yes," he said. "So sorry to have bothered you, Mr. Tanahill."

The curator leaned back on his desk. A slight grin crossed his craggy face. He had won the battle.

"Aye," he said. "Now it's best ye be on your way. I've work to do."

Colophon stood near the door to his office. "Mr. Tanahill, does the college have any books or pamphlets for sale about the college's silver collection?"

"Aye," he replied. "There are pamphlets for sale at the porter's lodge."

She turned to Julian. "Do we have time to stop by the porter's lodge and pick one up?"

"Uh, I guess so," Julian replied.

"Great!" She headed out of the office.

"Ye know," Tanahill said to Julian, "if all she wants is a pamphlet, ye could have saved me a lot of time."

Julian shrugged his shoulders. "Teenagers," he said. "What are you going to do?"

New Court
Corpus Christi College
Cambridge, England
Monday, June 11
3:30 p.m.

Julian and Colophon stepped out of the building that housed the college's offices and into New Court. They stood next to the college chapel and directly below the large red-faced clock.

"Okay," said Julian. "What's the plan?"

Colophon looked up at the clock. "Three minutes."

"Three minutes?"

"And I need your phone," she said. "It has a camera, right?"

"Yes, but why don't you use your . . ." He paused. Colophon's backpack was missing. "Where's your backpack?"

"Phone, please?"

Julian pulled his phone out of his satchel and

handed it to Colophon. "It's brand new," he said. "Be careful with it."

She examined his new smartphone. "Nice. This'll get the job done."

"What job?"

She looked back up at the clock. "Two and a half minutes." She pointed across the lawn. "You need to go to the porter's lodge. Mr. Tanahill will be there soon. Keep him there as long as you can." She walked over to the entrance to the chapel and stepped into the shadows.

"Go!" she said.

Norris Tanahill poured himself a cup of coffee, sat down at his desk, and thought, *A job well done.* He took pride in serving not only as the curator of the college's silver, but as its gatekeeper as well. He had turned away politicians, professors, and on one occasion, a duke of some sort or another. He grinned—a young girl and her keeper were no match for him.

He leaned forward to take a sip of coffee.

WEEEEEEOOOOOOOOO WEEEEEEEEEEEOOOOOOOOOO

The high, piercing noise filled the room. He spewed coffee all over his desk.

"What the—?"

WEEEEEEOOOOOOOOO WEEEEEEEEEEEOOOOOOOOOO

Was it a fire alarm? No, he realized, the emergency lights in his office were not flashing.

WEEEEEEOOOOOOOOO WEEEEEEEEEEOOOOOOOOOO

He checked his computer. Nothing.

WEEEEEEOOOOOOOOO WEEEEEEEEEEOOOOOOOOOO

He checked his hearing aid. Nope. It was working fine.

WEEEEEEOOOOOOOOO WEEEEEEEEEEOOOOOOOOOO

He stood up and walked around his desk in an effort to pinpoint the source of the sound.

WEEEEEEOOOOOOOOO WEEEEEEEEEEOOOOOOOOOO

The noise seemed to be coming from the far side of his desk.

WEEEEEEOOOOOOOOO WEEEEEEEEEEOOOOOOOOOO

He stared down at the floor in front of his desk.

A backpack.

WEEEEEEOOOOOOOOO WEEEEEEEEEEOOOOOOOOOO

The noise was coming from the backpack. He opened it and pulled out the source of the sound—a phone.

WEEEEEEOOOOOOOOO WEEEEEEEEEEOOOOOOOOOO

He pushed several buttons on the phone, but the noise would not stop.

WEEEEEEOOOOOOOOO WEEEEEEEEEEOOOOOOOOOO

"That infernal girl!" he growled.

WEEEEEEOOOOOOOOO WEEEEEEEEEEOOOOOOOOOO

He briefly considered crushing the phone to end the noise.

It would serve the girl right. Wouldn't be so forgetful next time, would she?

Then he reconsidered. The girl and her chaperone had managed to secure a private tour of the college. Maybe they knew someone important. Maybe *they* were important. Being rude was one thing (and practically expected in his unique position), but destroying a little girl's phone was quite another.

Drat it all.

He grabbed the phone and the backpack and headed into the hallway leading to New Court.

WEEEEEEOOOOOOOOO WEEEEEEEEEEEOOOOOOOOOO

Colophon stood in the deep shadows of the chapel's entrance, her back pressed hard against the stone wall. She checked to make sure Julian's phone was in silent mode, then looked at her watch.

Ten seconds . . . 9 . . . 8 . . . 7 . . . 6 . . . 5 . . . 4 . . . 3 . . . 2 . . . 1.

Thirty seconds later she heard the door to the administrative offices open to her right. A moment later she was looking at the back of Norris Tanahill as he huffed down the walkway in the direction of the porter's lodge. In his hand was her backpack. She slipped out of the shadows and made her way quickly to the offices' entrance.

Inside the porter's lodge Julian was discussing their tour of the college with Ashby Scolfield, as the head porter stood before a large window that overlooked New Court. No more than a couple of minutes after he entered the lodge, Julian looked out the window and saw the doors to the administrative offices burst open and Norris Tanahill emerge. The curator was visibly perturbed and was moving quickly along the courtyard in the direction of the porter's lodge. A moment or two later Colophon entered the administrative offices.

Colophon walked down the long hallway to Tanahill's office as quickly and as calmly as she could without drawing undue attention to herself. She had timed how long it took Julian to make his away around New Court and to the porter's lodge. At best she had three minutes to get in and out before Tanahill was back. Even then, she would be cutting it close.

She knew she had to avoid entanglements with Mr. Tanahill's fellow employees. It was not normal for a thirteen-year-old girl to stroll through the corridors of the college. The key, she decided, was to act as if she was supposed to be there, her age notwithstanding.

She was faced with this challenge almost immediately. As soon as she entered the hallway, she ran headlong into an older gentleman carrying an armload of books.

"So sorry," she said. "I'm in a bit of a hurry."

"Yes, well . . . " the man muttered. "Are you supposed—"

"I hope you're okay?" she interjected quickly.

"Well, yes—"

"Oh, thank goodness," she said cheerfully. "Best be off—can't be late, you know." And with that, she continued down the hallway.

The man paused momentarily, shrugged, then went on about his business. Colophon never looked back. Seconds later she reached the door to Tanahill's office. She glanced up and down the hallway.

It was empty.

She opened the door and slipped inside.

Norris Tanahill burst into the porter's lodge and slammed Colophon's backpack onto the desk between Julian and Ashby Scolfield.

WEEEEEEOOOOOOOOO WEEEEEEEEEEOOOOOOOOOO

"Where is the girl?" he demanded. "She needs to stop this infernal noise!"

Julian reached into Colophon's backpack and removed the phone.

WEEEEEEOOOOOOOOO WEEEEEEEEEEOOOOOOOOOO

He calmly took off the back cover and removed the battery. The alarm stopped immediately.

"No need to panic," he said. "Problem solved." He glanced out the window at the door to the administrative offices. Colophon was still inside.

"C'mon, Norris," said the head porter, "was all that fuss necessary? It's just a wee bit o' noise."

Tanahill pointed his finger at the head porter. "Don't ye be starting with me, Ashby Scolfield. I'll have none of it today."

Colophon moved quickly to the display case, located in a dark recess in the wall directly behind Tanahill's desk. The small silver box containing the quill sat in the middle of the case, surrounded by various other objects. The case did not appear to be locked or to have any type of alarm attached to it. Colophon grabbed the front of the display glass and attempted to lift it.

It didn't budge.

She examined the display case. There was no sign

of a lock. She tried once again. And again, it didn't budge.

She was running out of time.

Julian glanced across the courtyard at the large wooden door leading to the administrative offices. No sign of Colophon.

Tanahill, for his part, was continuing to berate the head porter over the interruption of his afternoon coffee.

Scolfield seemed to be taking it all in stride. "Care for a cup of tea instead?" he asked. "The water's hot."

"Tea?" exclaimed Tanahill. "Tea? For thirty years I've had a cup o' coffee every afternoon. And ye darn well know that!"

Julian glanced out again. Still no Colophon. He needed to do something to keep Tanahill here.

"Wow," said Julian. "Thirty years of coffee. That's . . . uh . . . quite impressive. Can I buy you a cup? We passed a Caffè Nero on our way from the train station—it's just down the street. We could pop in and grab a quick cup or two."

"I prefer to make my own coffee," replied Tanahill. "And I prefer to drink it alone."

Still no Colophon.

"I completely understand," Julian said. "I know I enjoy just sitting and thinking with a nice cup of coffee. Maybe a scone or a muffin of some sort. And a newspaper—a newspaper or magazine. Really refreshes the mind, don't you agree?"

Tanahill glared at him.

Still no Colophon.

"Do you take your coffee with cream and sugar?" Julian asked. "I like a bit of sweetness in mine—perhaps a nice hazelnut creamer?"

Stupid question, Julian thought.

"Cream and sugar?" said Tanahill. "Hazelnut creamer? Do I look like a wee little bairn to you?"

Julian took another quick glance into the courtyard. Still no Colophon.

"Black, then?" said Julian.

Another stupid question.

"Aye," replied Tanahill.

"Drip or press?" asked Julian.

Tanahill didn't answer but said to the head porter, "I'll be going now before he asks what type of filter I use." He turned and opened the door.

"Wait!" yelled Julian.

Tanahill looked at Julian. "Aye?"

Julian thought furiously of some question to ask,

something that would grab Tanahill's attention and delay his departure. Unfortunately, all that came out was: "Dark roast or medium?"

The door slammed shut behind him as Tanahill headed to the courtyard.

"He prefers a dark roast, I believe," said the head porter.

Colophon looked all over the display case but could not locate a lock or latch that would open it. The narrow silver box sat just inches from her face, but it might as well have been a mile away.

Nervy—Showing or requiring
courage and fortitude; bold.

CNN Center, Infirmary
Atlanta, Georgia
Monday, June 11
10:47 a.m.

Mull sat in a chair in the infirmary and stared at the ceiling. Barely an hour ago he had felt as if he was going to die. Now, aside from feeling tired, he was fine. The doctor suggested that it might have been a mild case of food poisoning exacerbated by the heat of the studio lights and the stress of being on national television. Mull wasn't convinced. He had suffered through bouts of food poisoning on more than one occasion. It usually took a full twenty-four hours, at a minimum, to recover. But here he sat, perfectly fine. No, it wasn't a case of food poisoning.

Still, he thought, a diagnosis of food poisoning could work to his advantage. Perhaps the network might give him another interview. And who knows, the whole episode might even generate a little sympathy.

Mull took his phone out of his coat pocket. He had placed it on silent prior to going into the studio. Now he had several missed calls and two texts. One of the messages was from Uncle Portis. It had arrived fifteen minutes ago. It read: "We have to speak IMMEDIATELY." The second message was also from Uncle Portis. It read simply: "I did all I could."

New Court, Corpus Christi College
Cambridge, England
Monday, June 11
3:50 p.m.

Julian stood inside the porter's lodge and watched helplessly as Tanahill made his way around the courtyard and through the large wooden door leading into the administrative offices. He had briefly considered tackling him but decided that a trip to jail would not serve anyone's interests. So he stared out the window and hoped that Colophon knew what she was doing.

Colophon had no idea what she was doing.

There was no lock.

No latch.

Nothing.

The display case would not open.

And her time was almost up.

Norris Tanahill stomped toward his office. His footsteps reverberated through the hallway.

Coffee's probably cold by now, he fumed.

The sound of footsteps caught Colophon off guard. They were moving fast and in the direction of the office in which she now sat crouched behind Norris Tanahill's desk.

The footsteps stopped just outside the door.

Colophon looked over the desk and could see the door handle turning.

She had nowhere to go.

✦ ✦ ✦

Tanahill stepped into his office, closed the door behind him, and sat down at his desk. He took a deep breath. His wife had told him that he was too old to get so worked up over every little thing. *Calm down,* she told him constantly. *You'll have a heart attack.*

He grunted. Perhaps she was right.

He closed his eyes and leaned back in his chair.

Colophon crouched as far under the display case as she could get. If Tanahill had bothered to look down before sitting at his desk, he almost certainly would have seen the tips of her shoes. As it was, she was trapped. The curator sat between her and the only way out of the office. All she could do was sit and listen as the old grump breathed in and out.

As Colophon's eyes adjusted to the darkness, she took a closer look at her cramped surroundings. There were a couple of paper clips, lots of dust, and a pen cap lying about under the display case. The wall behind her appeared to be solid stone, as was the floor. The back of Tanahill's large leather chair, directly in front of her, was almost touching the front of the display case. She looked up at the bottom of the case above her head. It appeared to be a solid piece of wood with bracing. Then she noticed something.

She paused.

It couldn't be.

But it was.

There, under the front-left corner of the display case, was a small black button set in a brass casement. She knew instantly what it was. She wanted to kick herself.

Julian stood outside the porter's lodge and stared across the courtyard. Still no sign of Colophon. The clock tower on the chapel showed that it was now 3:55 p.m. He decided that if she didn't come out the door in the next five minutes, he would go in after her.

Colophon considered her options, none of which was particularly appealing. Tanahill seemed to have made himself quite comfortable and did not appear to be in any hurry to move. Her legs were starting to cramp, and it was incredibly hot under the display case. She didn't know how much longer she could hold out in this position.

She listened closely as Tanahill breathed in and out.

She wished he'd been this relaxed when they'd met earlier.

The periods between breaths grew longer and longer—the breaths deeper and deeper.

And then suddenly he was snoring.

Julian made his way around the courtyard and stood in front of the chapel. He looked up at the clock. It was now 3:57 p.m. Three minutes to go.

Colophon listened intently.

The snoring was steady. Tanahill was out cold.

She inched her way forward until she was directly behind Tanahill's chair. She stopped and listened again. The snoring continued.

She moved her legs under and then behind her. There was about a two-foot gap between the base of Tanahill's chair and the side of the display case. She took a deep breath and then slowly slid herself forward until she was completely out from under the case. Tanahill didn't move.

Colophon stood up.

She knew that she should leave immediately. She could walk out the door right now, and Tanahill would never know that she had been in his office.

She knew that every second she stayed in the room increased her odds of getting caught.

She knew it would be almost impossible to open the display case without being detected.

But she knew she had to try.

Colophon edged as close to the case as she could. Stretching out with her right hand, she reached under the corner and found the button.

She paused. Tanahill snored deeply less than a foot from where she stood.

She pushed the button.

Click.

Colophon winced. Her breath left her. The sound seemed impossibly loud in the small room. If Tanahill didn't hear it, he would surely hear her heart pounding in her chest. She stood absolutely still.

But he didn't wake up. He shifted ever so slightly in his chair, grunted, and resumed snoring.

Colophon slowly breathed in and tried to calm her thumping heart.

The top of the display case had opened ever so slightly. She reached over, delicately lifted the top, and removed the silver box. She carefully let the top back down but did not let it latch shut. She took the box, moved to the far side of the desk, and knelt down on the floor. She could hear Tanahill snoring on the other side.

Colophon turned her attention back to the box. As Ms. Cadewaller had said, engraved on the top was a large ornate rendering of the Greek letter sigma. But that was not all. Engraved on the sides was a series of smaller symbols—four on each side.

AVIII	ZII	ΓVIII	ZV
ZIII	KIX	ZVIII	KIV
ΓII	ZVII	HI	IVIII
KV	ZIX	KVII	ZIV

More clues to solve, Colophon thought—and they didn't seem to be getting any easier.

But deciphering the symbols would have to come later.

She took Julian's phone out of her pocket and snapped several photos of the box. Then she removed the lid and peered inside.

Sitting inside the box on a bed of purple velvet was a quill, approximately seven inches long and silver. It was not tarnished in the least. Tanahill had obviously taken great care of it. One end of the quill was flat and had a circular opening. Colophon assumed that the quill's nib—the part that was actually used to write with—would be inserted into the opening. The quill tapered to a point at the far end.

But it was the middle of the quill that Colophon found particularly interesting. It was inscribed with five decorative bands, each in a distinct style. In addition, between the third and fourth bands were the words BEATI PACIFICI.

Colophon snapped several photos of the quill, rotated it, and snapped several more.

Then she carefully replaced the lid on the box. Again she stopped and listened. Tanahill was still snoring.

She got up on her knees and peeked over the edge of the desk. Tanahill had not moved. She rose to her feet and tiptoed back to the display case. Ever so slowly, she raised the glass lid and put the box back in its place. She then lowered the lid as far as it would go without latching shut. She knew she had been lucky that Tanahill had not woken up when the case was opened. No need to tempt fate again.

The clock tower struck four o'clock. Julian took one last look around the courtyard, then opened the door to the administrative offices and stepped inside.

Colophon moved back across the room toward the door. Her heart was racing. She glanced back over at Tanahill. He remained sound asleep.

She took two more steps.

Slowly, she told herself. *Don't rush.*

Two more steps.

She could feel her pulse rate slowing. She was almost out of the room.

She now stood directly in front of the office door.

She placed her right hand on the doorknob and started to turn it.

The voice boomed from behind her.

"AND WHAT MIGHT YE BE DOING IN MY OFFICE?"

Colophon turned around and stood face to face with Norris Tanahill.

Julian stood inside the doorway of the administrative offices. The hallway was empty. There was no sign of Colophon. Suddenly he heard the angry voice of Norris Tanahill thundering down the hallway. Julian broke into a sprint.

Colophon took a deep breath. Tanahill's face was bright red. "What are ye doing in my office?" he demanded again.

She looked directly at him as she tried to stay calm. "I've misplaced my backpack. I thought I might have left it in your office."

Tanahill's eyes narrowed into small slits. "That doesn't explain why ye'd be skulking around me office. Perhaps you were trying to get a peek at the quill?"

Her gaze never left his face. She knew that he would be looking for some sign that she was not telling the truth. She said as confidently as possible, "I wasn't skulking. You were sleeping, and I was trying not to disturb you."

Tanahill stared at her. He didn't seem to be buying her story.

"I'd best be going," she said. "I'm sure my cousin is looking for me by now."

Colophon turned to open the door. But Tanahill reached around her and put his hand over the doorknob. "Ye will not be going anywhere, young missy. Ye have a few more questions to answer."

Tanahill now appeared calm, determined, and serious. Colophon preferred him angry and red-faced.

"Now," he said, "let's have a little talk about—"

Knock knock.

The sound startled both of them. They turned and looked at the heavy wooden door.

Knock knock.

A voice from the other side of the door called out. "Hello? Mr. Tanahill?"

Julian.

Tanahill cracked opened the door and peered out.

"Oh, thank goodness you're here," Julian said. "I can't find Colophon anywhere. When she didn't return to the porter's lodge, I thought she might have come to your office to look for her backpack."

Tanahill looked over at Colophon and then back to Julian. "Aye. She's here." He opened the door wide, and Julian stepped inside.

With an anguished look, Colophon exclaimed to Julian, "My backpack is missing! I thought I must have left it in here, but I guess I was wrong. We need to keep looking."

Then she turned to Tanahill. "My mother will be so upset with me."

"Good news!" Julian held up the backpack. "And you have Mr. Tanahill to thank. He was kind enough to bring it to the porter's lodge when he realized you'd left it in his office."

Colophon looked at Tanahill. "Why didn't you tell me you'd found my backpack?"

The question caught the curator off guard. "Well, I . . . was . . ."

"You didn't tell her?" Julian said.

"Now, see here, I was . . . about . . . that infernal noise!" Tanahill stammered.

"Well, I must say that I'm terribly disappointed," said Julian. "Colophon must've been so worried."

"I was worried," said Colophon.

"I . . . in . . . my office . . . questions." Tanahill's face turned red from embarrassment.

Julian looked down at his watch and then back up at the curator. His voice was stern. "If we didn't have to catch a train, we would certainly discuss this matter further."

He handed Colophon her backpack. "Come, Colophon, we've a train to catch."

And before Tanahill could say another word, they had stepped out of his office and were headed down the hallway toward the courtyard.

The curator stood inside his office and contemplated what had just occurred.

I need a cup of coffee, he finally decided.

Chapter Seventeen
Rumination

Rumination — The act of thinking about
something in a sustained fashion.

Platform 2, Cambridge Rail Station
Cambridge, England
Monday, June 11
4:40 p.m.

Colophon and Julian sat on a bench awaiting the return train to London. During the taxi ride from the college to the train station, she had described for Julian how she had hidden in Tanahill's office and photographed the quill. Julian had admonished her for taking such a risk, but he could not hide how impressed he was by her courage and determination.

As they sat on the bench, Julian scrolled through the photographs of the quill on his camera. He easily translated the Latin phrase BEATI PACIFICI as "Blessed are the peacemakers."

"It's one of the most famous phrases from the Bible," he said. "And I know someone else who used it as well."

"Let me guess," said Colophon. "Shakespeare?"

"In *Henry the Sixth, Part Two*, to be exact," he replied.

"So another clue," she said. "And the other markings?"

Julian shrugged. "More clues, I suppose. But I have no idea what they mean."

She sensed a weariness about Julian. Something was clearly bothering him. "What's going on?"

He sighed. "I need to show you something."

He pulled a brown package from his bag and handed it to her.

"I found it in Wales."

Colophon carefully opened the package. Inside was a small leather book, obviously quite old. The title was *The troublefome raigne and lamentable death of Edward the fecond, King of England*. Beneath the title of the book was the symbol for sigma—Σ.

Julian took the book from Colophon, opened it to the final page, and handed it back to her. Colophon stared at the small engraving at the bottom of the page—it was the Letterford family crest—a crescent moon over crossed quills.

"What is this?" asked Colophon.

"It's a play," replied Julian. "The book you're holding was printed by Miles Letterford in 1622."

"I don't recognize it. Is it one of Shakespeare's plays?"

"No," he said. "It's by Christopher Marlowe."

"Marlowe?" she exclaimed. She looked at him. Why hadn't he told her about the book?

Julian said, "There's more."

"What?" Colophon asked.

Julian turned to the frontispiece—to the image of the hawk holding a spear. "I believe," Julian said, "that this is Shakespeare's coat of arms."

Julian sighed deeply. He could tell that Colophon was concerned and confused by this news. "I checked to see if the book was listed in the Stationers' Register," he said, "but it's not."

"The Stationers' Register?"

"The Stationers' Company was a trade guild in London," he replied. "It regulated the publishing trade and maintained a record—the register—of books that were published during the time Miles Letterford was alive. Every book that Miles Letterford published is listed in the register—apparently with one exception. It's clear that this book was never intended to be seen by the public."

"What does this mean?" she asked.

"I don't know," he said. "But I have a theory. Not even a theory really—a thought."

She gripped the book tightly. "Well, what is it?"

"You know that a lot of people believe William Shakespeare didn't write his own plays."

"I know," she said. "But the manuscripts we discovered proved that he really did write them."

"So it would seem," he said. "But how much do you really know about Shakespeare? I'm not talking about Shakespeare the writer. How much do you know about Shakespeare the person?"

She paused. "Not a lot, I suppose."

"Most people don't, and that's not particularly surprising. It's not as if he wrote an autobiography. For the most part, we know about Shakespeare from his plays, poems, and sonnets, which were magnificent. And that's part of the mystery of Shakespeare."

"What do you mean?" she asked. "What mystery?"

"Think about it," said Julian. "If you judged Shakespeare solely by his works, you would think he was a sophisticated, well-educated man of the world who had traveled extensively and could read and write in multiple languages."

"He wasn't?" asked Colophon.

"Hardly," he said. "Shakespeare was the son of a glove maker from a small rural town. His formal education was very limited, and he didn't attend university. He was married by the time he was eighteen years old, so he had to find some way to take care of his family. Exactly what he did before he showed up in London is anyone's guess. Some people think he might have been a country schoolmaster. But even if he was a schoolmaster—and that's a big *if*—it still doesn't explain how this simple man turned into the greatest playwright of all time."

"Maybe he learned about everything from books," suggested Colophon. "That's possible, isn't it?"

"It's possible," replied Julian. "But some people believe it's more likely that someone who was highly educated and well traveled wrote the plays."

She looked down at the book. "Someone like Marlowe."

"Well, that's what some people say."

"But why would Marlowe need to use Shakespeare's name? Didn't he already write plays?"

"Good point," he said. "Many of the other people who were allegedly the author of Shakespeare's plays had a reason not to be discovered. For example, Sir Francis Bacon was a prominent scientist and Lord Chancellor. Being a playwright was not the most reputable of professions back then. So a lot of people think Bacon may have used Shakespeare as a cover."

"But didn't Marlowe die in 1593? Isn't that what Ms. Cadewaller told us?"

Julian nodded. "You're correct."

"And when were Shakespeare's plays written?"

"Most of them were written after 1593," he replied.

Colophon crossed her arms. "Then that proves it. Marlowe couldn't have written the plays. He was dead."

Julian adjusted his glasses. "If, in fact, Marlowe was dead."

"What do you mean?"

"Ms. Cadewaller left out a few facts about Marlowe —facts that are particularly relevant to our search."

She moved to the edge of her seat. "What facts?"

"Do you recall from the brass plate on Marlowe's room how long he attended Corpus Christi College?"

She retrieved her notebook from her backpack and looked for her notes on the brass plate. "Seven years."

"Long time to complete college, don't you think?"

"Maybe he had a lot to do. Or he was a bad student."

"He did have a lot to do," said Julian. "He was a spy."

Colophon shot up off the bench. "A spy!" A young couple on the platform looked over at her.

Julian motioned for her to sit down.

"A spy?" she said. "Are you sure?"

"Actually," replied Julian, "it's quite well documented that he was a spy. He missed a lot of classes because of his . . . extracurricular activities for the Crown."

"Okay, so he was a spy—which is very cool, by the way. But what does that have to do with the Shakespeare theory? Marlowe was still dead when most of the plays were written."

"Or was he?" asked Julian. "Marlowe was a spy. People become spies for a lot of different reasons. Marlowe may have loved his country, but he also had a certain lifestyle to maintain. He enjoyed the good life—good food, good drink, and good times. The money he made from spying paid for that lifestyle."

"So he spent a lot of money. What does that have to do with his death?"

"Coly, think about it. What if the French or Spanish

had offered Marlowe even more money? Or in England itself—there were constant plots against the Crown. A spy would have been very useful in those circumstances—for the right price, of course."

"Marlowe was a double agent?"

"Not that we know of," said Julian. "But that's always the risk with a spy, isn't it? Marlowe lived in dangerous times. A lot of men and women lost their head to the sword based on nothing more than a rumor. Marlowe may have known his time was short."

"Wait a second. Are you saying he faked his death?"

"Do you know how Marlowe allegedly died?"

Colophon shook her head. Ms. Cadewaller had only said he died much too young.

"He died in a fight in a tavern," said Julian. "But the specific cause of death was a dagger in the face."

"Gross."

"I agree," said Julian. "Gross and convenient. It's hard to identify a face under those circumstances."

Colophon sat silent for a moment. "But what about the body? How could he fake that?"

Julian scooted close to her. His voice was little more than a whisper. "The evening before Marlowe was allegedly stabbed, a man by the name of John Penry died. Penry was approximately the same age, height, and weight as Marlowe. The night Penry died, his body vanished."

"Vanished?"

"Gone," said Julian. "Never to be seen again. So we had two deaths in two days, but only one body was buried."

"So couldn't someone just dig up Marlowe's grave and conduct some sort of DNA test? That would prove whether he's buried there or not. They do it all the time on TV."

"Perhaps," he replied. "But the authorities buried him in an unmarked grave. No one knows exactly where he's buried."

"An unmarked grave?" asked Colophon. "That's a strange way to treat someone so famous."

"Yes," said Julian. "And again, very convenient, don't you think?"

The train for London was pulling into the station. They gathered their bags and headed down the platform.

"So," she said, "if Marlowe faked his death, he could've written Shakespeare's plays."

"That's the theory," replied Julian.

"But why would Shakespeare go along with that?" she asked.

"For fame and fortune," he said. "If Shakespeare was just a simple, poorly educated man from a small town, wouldn't this seem like a great idea? Shakespeare becomes famous and rich—and all he has to do is pass off Marlowe's plays as his own."

Colophon remained silent as they entered the train and found their seats. She looked out the window at the passengers scurrying about on the platform. After several minutes, the train started moving.

"Julian?"

Julian, who had been texting copies of the photographs to Colophon's phone, looked up. "Yes?"

"If we keep searching, are we going to prove that Shakespeare wrote the manuscripts . . . or that Marlowe wrote them?"

He put down his phone and stared out the window. "I don't know, Coly. I just don't know."

International Terminal
Hartsfield-Jackson International Airport
Atlanta, Georgia
11:45 a.m.
Monday, June 11

The man's phone had started vibrating in his coat pocket almost the moment he arrived at the airport terminal. He pulled his phone out of his coat. He had fifteen new text messages.

He opened the first one. It was a picture of a silver box. He looked at the next message — another picture of the same box. And the next two photographs were the same. The fifth picture, however, was different — some sort of long, thin silver object. It was covered with unusual markings and seemed to be engraved with text.

A pen perhaps?

The photos that followed all seemed to be different views of the same silver object.

He had been somewhat unsure about the decision to monitor the girl's cell phone. It wasn't that it was particularly difficult to have the girl's phone tapped. Technology had certainly made his job easier at times. Rather, he thought, it was a waste of time and effort. She was, after all, just a thirteen-year-old girl who had gotten lucky when she uncovered the secret crypt under the church in Stratford-upon-Avon and unlocked the key to finding the Shakespeare manuscripts.

But his employer disagreed.

We're not taking any chances, he was told.

So for the last week he had monitored every call,

e-mail, and text she had sent or received. After days of reading useless e-mails and messages, he realized that she finally seemed to be on the trail of something.

Trigue James forwarded the photographs to Treemont.

CHAPTER EIGHTEEN
Gloomy

Gloomy—Marked by hopelessness;
very pessimistic.

Manchester, Georgia
Monday, June 11
8:37 p.m.

Case Letterford sat in the dugout. The teams, families, and fans had long departed. Rick Parker, Case's coach and the father of his best friend, had just finished dragging the infield. The dust still lingered in the air.

Case, who was staying with the Parker family until baseball season was over, had asked Mr. Parker if he could hang out at the field before heading over to the Parkers' home on Third Avenue.

"Sure," Mr. Parker had said. "Just don't let it get too dark."

Case had assured him that he would be there soon.

They had all seen what had happened on CNN that morning. But no one said anything to Case about it. Even the players on the opposing team kept quiet. No trash talk. Nothing. Case's father was well respected and well liked in Manchester. So everyone simply pretended that nothing had happened.

But Case could see it in their eyes. He could see it in the way they quickly turned when he caught them staring at him.

As if that were not bad enough, Case would be turning sixteen soon, yet it was his younger sister who had headed off to England to try, once again, to save the family business. His father, despite what had happened on national television, was also trying to do something. His mother was diligently assisting in the research on the manuscripts. Everyone seemed to be doing something to save the Letterford family—everyone except him.

The dust had now settled across the field. The sun had dropped below the thick stand of pine trees behind the outfield fence. The crickets had started their nightly chorus.

"I heard you got two hits tonight."

Case turned around. It was his father.

"One hit and a fielder's choice," Case replied.

"You got on base," said Mull Letterford. "That's what counts."

"I suppose," said his son.

Mull sighed. "I should've been here to see you play."

"You were busy."

"Did you see it?" Mull asked.

"Everyone saw it," Case replied.

"I'm sorry."

Case stood up and faced his father. "You shouldn't be sorry," he said. "You were at least trying to do something. All I did was play baseball."

"Maybe it would have been better if I had played baseball and let you go on television."

"No," said Case. "I've seen you play baseball. You're terrible."

Mull laughed. "I needed that. It's been a long day."

Case gathered up his glove and bat, and Mull and Case started toward the parking lot.

"There's something we need to talk about," Mull said.

CHAPTER NINETEEN

Dishearten

Dishearten—To cause to lose hope
or enthusiasm; dispirit.

Letterford residence
Clerkenwell, London, England
Tuesday, June 12

Colophon woke up just as the morning was starting
to make its way through the shades in her room. She

lay in her bed and watched the dust dance and float through the beams of sunlight streaming through her window. She didn't want to get out of bed—at least not yet. But she knew that she would eventually have to face all the new questions brought about by her trip to Cambridge the previous day.

Was Marlowe really Shakespeare?

Who was the real author of the manuscripts that she and Julian had found?

What did all the markings on the quill box and quill mean?

Colophon pulled the cover up over her head—the day could wait for just a little while longer. She had started with one clue—a simple inkwell. That simple clue had led her to Corpus Christi College, Christopher Marlowe, and the Matriculation Quill. The mysterious Latin phrase on the inkwell had given way to an equally enigmatic Latin phrase on the quill—BEATI PACIFICI—"Blessed are the peacemakers."

Was she getting close to proving that the Shakespeare manuscripts were real—or further away?

And then there was her father's appearance on CNN. Her mother had told her about it when she returned from Cambridge yesterday. Meg had described it as "unfortunate." Colophon didn't think that sounded so bad. Then she saw the video on You-Tube. It wasn't unfortunate—it was an unmitigated disaster. Her father was pale and shaking. Sweat dripped from his forehead. Colophon could barely watch.

The press coverage was even worse. Her father was described variously as nervous, evasive, untrustworthy, deceitful, a liar, and a dissembler. No one bothered to mention the obvious—that he was clearly very ill. Of course, some of the news coverage also felt obligated to include the video of her father being chased by dogs in New York City the previous December. All things considered, she decided, another fifteen minutes or so in the warmth and comfort of her bed wouldn't hurt.

Finally she managed to pull herself out of bed, shower, and eat a bit of breakfast. She then spent the rest of the morning searching the Internet to find out anything she could about the markings and inscription on the quill.

Julian, who had returned to Wales for a couple of days, would have laughed at her approach to solving this clue.

"The Internet is no substitute for real research," he would have said yet again.

And he was right. But that didn't mean it wasn't worth trying.

After lunch, to cheer herself up, Colophon spent an hour or so e-mailing her friends at home and at camp. According to Lyla McRae, a friend unfortunate enough to be stuck at Camp Arrowhead, it had rained there for five straight days. Colophon felt a bit guilty for leaving Lyla alone. Like Colophon, Lyla was not one of the popular kids at camp. It was always good to have a friend under those circumstances. Still, Lyla seemed to be holding up reasonably well. Colophon was reading through her hilarious account of archery lessons in a torrential downpour when her mother called for her to come downstairs.

"Be right there!" Colophon yelled. She closed her laptop and headed down to the kitchen. To her surprise, she found her father sitting at the kitchen table with her mother.

"Dad!" Colophon exclaimed as she ran over and hugged him. "What are you doing here?"

Mull Letterford hugged Colophon tight. "I just needed to see my favorite daughter."

She sat down in a chair next to her father. "Rough week, huh?"

"You could say that."

In all of the excitement over seeing her father, Colophon hadn't paid any attention to her mother, who was now standing by the kitchen sink. But one glance was enough—Colophon could tell that her mom had been crying.

Colophon looked at her dad. "What's wrong?"

Mull placed his hand on his daughter's knee. "You've seen the CNN interview?"

"Yes."

"It didn't go well."

Colophon nodded. She clasped her hands together.

"After the interview," Mull said, "the family had a meeting to discuss . . . the situation. A vote was taken. Circumstances have now changed."

Colophon couldn't speak. Her mouth felt as if it was filled with sand.

"The family," Mull continued, "voted to remove me as the owner of the company."

No one said a word. The only sounds were the gentle hum of the refrigerator and the faint *click click click* of the second hand on the kitchen clock.

"How *could* they?" Colophon finally exclaimed. Didn't they know how much her father had done for the company?

Mull gripped Colophon's hands. She could see the strain in his eyes. He seemed exhausted. "They did what they thought was for the best of the company." He did not sound convincing.

"But who will be the owner?" She already knew the answer.

"Treemont," her father replied. "I turned the family key over to him before I left."

Tears started to flow down Colophon's face. The key had been a part of her family for her entire life. It had sat on her father's desk and her grandfather's desk. She couldn't bear the thought of Treemont owning it.

"What about our home in Manchester?" Colophon asked.

"It now belongs to Treemont," said her father. "Our belongings are being placed in storage for us."

"But where will we live?"

"Right here, in London," her father replied. "Uncle Portis convinced the family that we should be permitted to keep this house."

Colophon contemplated this news. Her friends, her school, her entire life was back in the United States.

"Does Case know?" she asked.

"I told him yesterday," he replied. "Baseball season's almost over. He's going to fly over with your aunt Audrey in just a few days."

"And Maggie? Treemont doesn't get our dog too, does he?" She knew she sounded like a little girl asking this, but she didn't care.

"No," Mull said. "Maggie's our dog. She's staying with the Parkers. We're making arrangements to have her sent over."

Meg Letterford sat down next to Colophon and hugged her. "It'll be all right," she said. "We'll be together as a family. I know you don't want to leave your friends and your school and your home. I know that. But I promise it'll be okay."

Colophon buried her head in her mother's arms and cried.

Manchester, Georgia
Wednesday, June 13

The furniture in the library of the former Letterford residence had been pushed to the side of the room. A large Smart Board on an aluminum stand now dominated the space. A series of cables and wires ran from the back of the board into the adjoining hallway. A slight humming emanated from the board.

To the side of the Smart Board and sitting on a metal tripod was the portrait of Miles Letterford. Two sets of studio lights had been set up in front of the painting.

Treemont approached the board and tapped the bottom left-hand corner. A series of photographs immediately appeared on the board. Treemont touched one of the photographs and moved it to the middle of the board. He tapped the photograph twice, and it expanded to fill the screen. He then turned to face the man and the woman who stood behind him.

He pointed at the photograph. "I need to know everything there is to know about this object." He gestured at a stack of boxes in the corner of the room. "Everything you need to know about Miles Letterford is in those boxes." He pointed to the books on the shelves. "Every book that Miles Letterford ever published is in this room. Some are well over four hundred years old. Many cannot be replaced. Tear them apart if you must."

Finally he pointed to the portrait of Miles Letterford. "I know he has more secrets to tell. I want to know what they are."

The man and the woman nodded. They knew they had a lot of work to do.

PART II

"When a man's verses cannot be understood, nor a man's good wit seconded with the forward child understanding, it strikes a man more dead than a great reckoning in a little room."

William Shakespeare, *As You Like It,* act 3, scene 3

Prologue

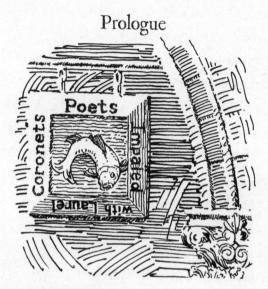

The Mermaid Tavern
Bread Street, London, England
Late afternoon
June 1, 1593

"Marlowe is dead!"

The news echoed through the dark interior of the tavern. The men gathered in the room turned toward the door. The room went silent save for the crackling of the fireplace and the dull clank of pewter cups.

Thomas Runford stepped inside and repeated his news. "Marlowe is dead!"

"A foul rumor!" proclaimed a voice.

"Nay, 'tis true," insisted Runford. "The craven deed

occurred at Bull's House in Deptford. A drunken fight. Stabbed through the eye, I heard."

An unnamed voice from the far reaches of the tavern declared that such slanderous comments about Marlowe demanded the Drunkard's Cloak—and others suggested more grievous punishments.

But Runford persisted. He had heard the news from his cousin, a cordwainer in Deptford, who had heard the news from his brother, who had seen the body of Marlowe.

This statement elicited yet another round of animated comments about Runford, many of which were pointed enough to convince the messenger that it would be best to leave the tavern. The discussion, however, continued long after Runford's departure. Most of the room's occupants continued to express doubt over the veracity of the news and outrage at the messenger who had dared to besmirch Marlowe's name. This would not be the first time, many noted, that news of a death had carried itself across London only to later be proven false. Many a man had been declared dead at sundown, only to reappear the next morning in perfect health. And several others noted that it was not the first time Marlowe's name had been cast about in such an ill manner.

One man, however, was certain that the news about Marlowe was true. William Shakespeare sat alone at a table in a dark recess of the tavern and listened to the low murmur of the tavern's patrons. Marlowe was dead—of that Shakespeare had little doubt. But he knew Marlowe had not died in a drunken brawl. Although Marlowe's general character and reputation lent great weight to the truth of the rumor, Shakespeare knew otherwise.

And he had known this day might come.

Now it was here. Now it was time.

His thought was interrupted by the loud clank of cups on the table. "Shall I leave you to ponder, old friend? Or will you join me in wine?" Miles Letterford sat down at the table across from Shakespeare without waiting for an answer.

"It seems wine has brought us far more than we expected this day."

"I take no heed of such rumors," replied Miles. "They spread like the plague—and, it seems, bring death in equal measure."

"Perhaps," said Shakespeare, "but I fear this rumor casts long the darkness and the gloomy shade of death."

"Then we raise our cup to Marlowe," said Miles Letterford.

Shakespeare picked up the cup of wine. His thoughts were of preparations to be made, lest he or others suffer Marlowe's fate. He raised his cup. "Aye," he replied. "To Marlowe."

Chapter Twenty
Vulnerable

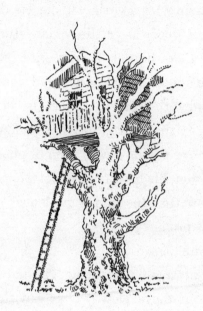

Vulnerable—Susceptible to physical harm or
damage; susceptible to emotional injury.

Manchester, Georgia
Thursday, June 14
7:30 a.m.

Past the stacked stone wall, across the field, and hidden deep in the branches of a large and ancient oak was a small treehouse. Case and his father had built it when Case was nine years old. It had served as his refuge ever since. A window looked out over the pasture toward the house.

Case had built shelves out of scrap pieces of wood and filled them with a variety of objects that he had found in the woods over the years—turtle shells, antlers, old Coke bottles, acorns, interesting rocks, and railroad spikes. The opposite wall was filled from top to bottom with posters and pictures of every size and variety. In the top-right corner—almost hidden by a *Star Wars* poster—was a small photograph of Case, his father, his mother, and Colophon.

Case knew that his family no longer owned the house or the property.

But he didn't care.

It would always be his home. He had learned to ride a bike in the driveway that ran through the pasture. He had broken his arm in a fall from the hickory tree that stood just outside the window to his room. And he had sat in this very treehouse for countless hours and read comic books, listened to music, napped, and escaped from the world.

Colophon had her persimmon tree. Case had his treehouse.

Two days ago Case had sneaked across the back side of the property and over to the treehouse. He was going to be leaving for England soon, and he just wanted to sit there for a little while and forget about everything that had happened. He had expected the main house to be empty—the movers had already packed up most of the family's belongings and put them in storage. But he had been surprised to see cars arriving at and leaving the house. Treemont, he had understood from his father, had no interest in living in Manchester. But it sure looked like someone was doing something at the house. Case was too far away to tell exactly what.

He considered texting his sister and telling her about it. But he knew what her response would be.

"Find out what's going on," she would say. And he was already determined to do just that.

So Case now found himself sitting in the treehouse just before dawn and staring through a telescope he had borrowed from the Parkers. Mr. Parker and his father had grown up together in Manchester and had played in the woods where Case's treehouse now stood. Mr. Parker, who remained one of his father's closest friends, hadn't asked why Case needed the telescope or where he was headed at such an early hour. He just told Case to be careful and to call if he needed help.

Case had arrived before sunrise, set up the telescope in the window facing the house, and waited.

Shortly after nine a.m., the first car arrived. He recognized it from two days ago. Case peered through the telescope. It was Treemont, accompanied by two men in dark suits. Treemont exited his car and headed inside. The two men walked around the house and then got back in the car and sat in the driveway.

A rental car carrying a man and a woman arrived a half hour later. They went inside the house before Case could get a good look at their faces.

He turned the telescope to the library windows on the front of the house. The wooden shutters were partially shut and the glare from the rising sun made it difficult to see, but Case caught glimpses of movement in the library. Someone was definitely in there.

He sat down in the small folding chair he kept in the treehouse. He knew that to find out exactly what was going on, he would have to get into the house. That could prove tricky. The men in the car appeared to be security guards. And he had only a couple of days left before he would be on a plane to England. Time was not on his side. But he also knew that he had a distinct advantage. He had grown up in that house. He knew every crevice, casement, corner, and closet. If anyone could break into the house undetected, it was he.

And that was when Case heard someone speaking.

He couldn't quite make out what was being said, but the voice seemed to be coming from the pasture.

He peeked through the window.

One of the men from the car was walking across the field in his direction. His heart jumped in his chest.

Had the security guard seen the treehouse?

No.

Case knew that it was impossible to see the treehouse from the driveway during the summer. The thick foliage and deep shadows obscured any view of it.

And then it occurred to him. They hadn't seen the treehouse—they had seen the sun glinting off the lens of the telescope. He might as well have been yelling at them with a bullhorn and waving a flag.

Now he was trapped. If he climbed out of the treehouse and made a run for it, they'd see him. The canopy of the woods was thick—but that same thick foliage had long since stunted any undergrowth that could have hidden him.

CHAPTER TWENTY-ONE
Discontent

Discontent—A restless longing
for better circumstances.

Letterford residence
Clerkenwell, London, England
Thursday, June 14
4:00 p.m.

"Coly!" yelled Meg Letterford. "Come downstairs. We're going for a walk."

Colophon had spent much of the last two days moping about the house or holed up in her room.

They had been the worst two days of her life. Her whole world had been turned upside down. Her home was in Manchester, Georgia—not London, England. So much of what mattered to her was gone —the persimmon tree in the field, the bench near the lake where she would sit and read for hours, the doorframe in her bedroom where her father had measured and marked her height every year on her birthday.

She had no desire to take a walk. All she wanted to do was sit in her room.

But Meg Letterford was persistent.

"Coly! This is not a request. We have to get to the train station to pick up Maggie!"

Colophon jumped to her feet. *Maggie!*

She missed her golden retriever so much. She threw on her shoes and bounded down the stairs. Her mother was waiting in the foyer.

"I thought that might get your attention," her mother said. "We have to pick up Maggie at five-thirty at Victoria Station."

"That's a long way to walk," Colophon said.

"I think a long walk is in order," her mother replied, and headed out the front door.

Colophon hustled to catch up with her.

They walked several blocks without saying a word.

"I know you have questions," Meg finally said. "Ask them."

Colophon did have questions. For two days every conceivable scenario had played through her mind.

"Will we be okay?" she asked at last. "I know parents always say everything will be okay, but will we?"

Meg's response was firm and certain. "We'll be fine."

"But what about your job?"

"I'm going to Oxford tomorrow to discuss a position as a visiting professor. I hope you don't mind tagging along, but your father has . . . other matters to attend to."

"I don't mind," Colophon replied. She really had no choice. Julian had not yet returned from Wales, and her father had been in and out of the house for the last two days.

"What about Dad? What will he do?"

"He was offered a position with Letterford and Sons, but he just couldn't accept it. He said he couldn't bear the thought of working for Treemont." Meg cleared her throat. "So your father has . . . well . . . he's accepted a position as an editor with a newspaper here in London."

"That's great!" Colophon replied. "Is it the *Times*? Or the *Standard*?"

"No, not quite."

"The *Daily Mirror*?"

"No."

"The *Sun*?"

"No."

Colophon was exasperated. "Then exactly which newspaper?"

"The *London Scoop*."

Colophon stopped walking. "The *Scoop*? Did you just say the *Scoop*?"

"Yes."

"But that can't be right," Colophon said. "Isn't that the newspaper that insists the prime minister is an alien?"

"That would be the one."

"And that dinosaurs still live in Wales?"

"Yes."

"And that Canada doesn't really exist?"

It was Meg Letterford's turn to be exasperated. "Yes, that's the one. The owner of the *Scoop* is a friend of your father's from college. Your father needs a job until everything gets settled, and his friend is willing to help out."

Colophon knew it was difficult for her father. But taking a job at the *Scoop* told her just how bad things were.

"Sorry," Colophon said apologetically.

Meg put her arm over her daughter's shoulder. "What do you say we go get Maggie and welcome her home?"

Chapter Twenty-Two
Viewless

Viewless — Providing no view.

Manchester, Georgia
Thursday, June 14
11:15 a.m.

The man in the dark suit stood at the base of the large oak tree. "I told you I saw something shining in the woods," he whispered into a small walkie-talkie. "It's a treehouse."

"Check it out," said the voice in his earpiece. "Mr. Treemont told us not to take any chances."

The man clipped the walkie-talkie to his belt and slowly climbed the wooden ladder up to a small porch, then carefully eased himself onto it. He paused to catch his breath and listen for any sign of movement.

Nothing.

The door to the treehouse was closed, so the man gave it a slight nudge. It did not appear to be locked. He pushed it in.

"It's empty," the man said into his walkie-talkie. "Just a bunch of old junk—posters and rocks and stuff."

"Can you tell what was shining?" the voice in the earpiece asked. "Is there any sign of a camera or surveillance equipment?"

The man walked over and plucked a glass Coke bottle off the window ledge.

"It was a bottle," the man said. "Just the sun shining off a bottle."

"Great work. Are you going to bring it in to be questioned?"

"You're quite the comedian," the man replied. "Did you want to explain to Mr. Treemont that we saw something and didn't check it out?"

"No," said the voice. "But I suggest we keep this piece of detective work to ourselves."

"Agreed." The man stepped back onto the porch and prepared to climb down the ladder. "I'll be back in a couple of minutes."

Case could hear the creaking of the ladder as the man descended. He heard the thud of the man's feet hitting the ground and then the soft crunch of footsteps walking through the woods and into the field. Case lay perfectly still on the roof of the treehouse, the telescope at his side. His father had warned him on numerous occasions not to climb up on the roof, but he didn't think his father would mind in this particular instance.

Although he had heard only one side of the conversation, the man in the dark suit was clearly convinced that the Coke bottle had caused the reflection. Still, they now knew about the treehouse. They might decide to come by and check on it periodically. It would be too much of a risk to return to the treehouse. And, Case decided, if he was going to take a risk, it was going to be a really, really big one. But first he needed to convince Mr. Parker to let him retrieve something from the facility where his family's possessions were being stored.

✦ ✦ ✦

Maggie jumped up onto the bed, plopped down at Colophon's side, and promptly fell asleep. Colophon reached over, patted the golden retriever lightly on the head, then turned back to her laptop. Her mother had been right—a walk was just what she had needed. She had spent too much time feeling sorry for herself over the last few days. Maybe the family business had been taken away from her father. Maybe her whole life had been rearranged. But that didn't mean there weren't still clues to be followed. She knew the manuscripts were real, and she was more determined than ever to prove it.

She decided that if she was going to spend a day in Oxford, she might as well make it productive. Oxford, she knew, was the home of Oxford University. The town was filled with colleges, churches, libraries, theaters, lecture halls, and ancient buildings of every size and shape. It certainly seemed like fertile ground for clues. Colophon Googled the names Letterford and Oxford together to see if anything turned up. The search produced more than five thousand results.

Yikes, she thought.

She skimmed over the first few pages. Most of the results had nothing to do with either Oxford University or Miles Letterford. She had not realized how many cities were named Oxford.

There was Oxford, Alabama.

Oxford, Ohio.

Oxford, North Carolina.

There was also an Oxford, Georgia—which was news to Colophon.

And even the results that appeared to be somewhat relevant did not seem like particularly good leads. A bookstore on High Street in Oxford—the one in England—had a long list of books published by Letterford & Sons, but so did thousands of other bookstores around the globe in cities that were not named Oxford.

She yawned and glanced at the clock on her nightstand. It was late, and she was getting tired. She scrolled through several more pages of results—and just as she was about to give up and go to bed, one result caught her eye. It was a website for a place called the Bodleian Library at Oxford University.

At least it's in the right city.

She clicked on the link. It led to a list of the library's major donors and benefactors over the centuries. She scrolled down the list until, near the bottom of the page, she found the donors from the seventeenth century and the name she was looking for: Miles Letterford. To her disappointment, however, the list was just a list. It did not provide any details as to what her ancestor might have donated, when he might have donated it, or what connection he might have had to the library.

Not much to go on, she thought. Then again, when had that ever stopped her?

CHAPTER TWENTY-THREE

Multitudinous

Multitudinous—Consisting of many
parts; populous; crowded.

Paddington Station
London, England
Friday, June 15
8:35 a.m.

Colophon looked up at the large electronic display above the ticket office. It flickered constantly with updates on arrivals and departures. The train for Oxford was scheduled to leave at 8:51 a.m., but a platform had yet to be assigned. The train's status was listed as "on time." A large group of men and women stood below the display sipping their coffees and waiting. No one spoke. A voice on the intercom announced final call for the train to Banbury on platform three, echoing through the cavernous station.

The electronic display flickered once more. The train for Heathrow was now loading on platform six. As if a starting gun had been shot off, a large portion of the crowd immediately broke away and headed en masse toward platform six. Their spots were quickly filled by another group of coffee sippers anxiously watching the names and numbers flicker across the display.

To Colophon's right, a large ornate clock hung over the entrance to the station. It told her it was now 8:37 a.m. She took a sip of her hot chocolate and turned to her mother. "What time is your meeting?"

"One-thirty," replied Meg Letterford. "We'll have some time to kill once we arrive, so I thought we could wander around the town a bit and then have some lunch."

"After lunch," Colophon said, "could I take a tour of the Bodleian Library? You know—while you're in your interview? There's a two-hour tour that begins at one o'clock."

"The Bodleian Library?"

"It's the oldest library at Oxford University," replied Colophon, who had stayed up far too late reading about its history. "It's over five hundred years old. The place is supposed to be really incredible."

"I'm familiar with the Bodleian," replied her mother. "I'm a professor, remember? But are you up for two hours? It's not the kind of library you just sit in and read for fun."

"I understand," said Colophon. "It just seemed liked a neat place to visit—lots of history and stuff. And it's better than sitting in a stuffy waiting room while you have your interview."

The electronic display flickered. The train for Oxford was now loading on platform four.

"I suppose," said Meg, "I could spare you for a couple of hours."

Colophon grabbed her backpack and walked with her mother toward platform four.

"Now, about lunch," Colophon said. "Maybe we could find someplace that serves pizza?"

Chapter Twenty-Four
Dawn

Dawn—A first appearance; a beginning.

Manchester, Georgia
Friday, June 15
8:00 a.m.

Case had arrived back at his family's old property before dawn and hidden in a small stand of woods near the side of the house. There was only one way to find out what Treemont was doing—get into the house. He had briefly considered breaking in before Treemont arrived, but the house had a security system. A quick peek inside the front door told Case that the red activation light on the security keypad was glowing. That meant the system was armed. Case knew the code, but what if Treemont had changed it? It would be a risk. If the alarm went off, Treemont might increase the security or abandon the house altogether. There was too much uncertainty. He would have to wait until the house was occupied.

Case had seen Treemont's car coming up the driveway at a little before eight. As soon as it turned out of his view, Case grabbed his backpack and sprinted from the woods to a small window at the rear of the house, just above ground level. It led to the mechanical room. He knew that the window had never latched properly. His family had used it on more than one occasion when they found themselves locked out of the house. Case waited until he heard the front door close and counted to ten. Then he gave the window a slight push. It opened wide. He dropped his backpack to the floor below and slipped quietly inside. He needed to move quickly before the men with Treemont made their way around the house.

Case carefully shut the window and moved to the

far side of the room. He sat down behind a stack of boxes and took several deep breaths.

Calm down, he told himself. *You're inside.*

The room was dark and cool. The hot water heater gurgled, hummed briefly, and then shut off. The house was otherwise silent.

Case's eyes slowly adjusted to the darkness. To his right was a door that led to the basement. To his left—hidden behind a stack of boxes—was a small access panel that led to the crawlspace beneath the front of the house. He grabbed his backpack and headed for the panel.

Bodleian Library
Oxford, England
Friday, June 15
1:00 p.m.

A short, stout middle-aged woman stood on a small stool beside the security desk in the entrance hall of the Bodleian Library and waved her arms. "Gather round, gather round," she called in a disconcertingly deep voice. "Please hurry; we have much to see this morning." The tourists who were scattered throughout the hall immediately clustered around her.

Meg Letterford stood near the entrance with her

daughter. "All right, it's time for you to go," she said. "I'll see you back here at three."

"Good luck with your interview," Colophon said.

"Thanks. And have fun."

"Young lady!" the stout woman yelled in Colophon's direction. "Are you joining us this morning?" The small crowd turned in unison and looked at Colophon.

"Yes ma'am," she said as she hustled toward the group. She took one last glance back at her mother and waved.

"Now," said the woman on the stool, "as I was getting ready to say, welcome to the Bodleian Library! I am Anne Flynn, your tour guide for this morning. The Bodleian Library is actually made up of a variety of different buildings and facilities, several of which we will visit during the course of this tour. Duke Humfrey's Library, Radcliffe Camera, the Divinity School, the Tower of the Five Orders, and the quadrangle behind you are all part of the Bodleian Library complex."

Colophon remembered what Julian had said the previous December in Stratford-upon-Avon—that the next clue was probably right in front of them. And he had been right. She would need to pay close attention.

Ms. Flynn stepped off her stool and proceeded toward a stairway at the far end of the entrance hall. "We will begin our tour this morning in Duke Humfrey's Library," she said. "It was built in 1488 to house a collection of manuscripts donated by the Duke of Gloucester. Even though it's part of the Bodleian Library, it still bears the good duke's name."

The small crowd followed Anne Flynn past a security desk and up a set of marble stairs to the first landing. Once everyone had gathered there, Ms. Flynn pointed out the window to the quadrangle below. "As you can see, the building we are in wraps around the entire quadrangle. Most of the building is still used by students, fellows, and researchers. For example, the second and third floors—which are not part of the tour—are known as the Upper and Lower Reading Rooms."

As if on cue, a student came out of a door at the top of the next landing—the entrance to the Lower Reading Room—and made his way down through the tour group to the exit below.

Ms. Flynn waited until the student had passed, and then resumed. "We'll now proceed up to Duke Humfrey's Library. We'll spend a few minutes looking around and then regroup. And remember," she said, "don't touch any of the books."

Colophon and the rest of the group followed her up the stairs to a door on the second landing. Ms. Flynn held the door open as the tour group filed into the room. With her free hand, the tour guide held a finger to her lips and whispered "Be quiet" as each member of the group edged past her.

Colophon waited patiently as the people in front of her slowly worked their way through the doorway. She could hear gasps of amazement from inside the room. Colophon expected Ms. Flynn to be angry—she had, after all, warned them to be quiet. But to her surprise, Ms. Flynn was actually smiling—as if she expected the group to respond as they did.

Colophon was skeptical. It was just a library. How impressive could it be?

And then she stepped through the doorway and into the room.

It was remarkable.

It was two stories high, narrow and long. Despite the large arched windows at both ends of the room and in the wall facing out to the quadrangle, the room was dark—but in a comforting and warm way. Tones of amber, ochre, and crimson predominated. The room was filled from floor to ceiling with ancient books of every size, shape, and color. The uppermost books—far beyond the reach of even the tallest library ladder—were accessed by a rickety wooden walkway that skirted the room's perimeter, supported by wooden columns. Beneath the walkway and hidden in the shadows behind the columns were dark wooden desks and benches that ran the length of each wall.

The ceiling was constructed of large wooden beams, painted with colorful and fantastic images of animals, human heads, and strange swirling shapes. The spaces between the beams were filled with row after row of wooden panels—each decorated with a crest or coat of arms of some sort.

"Wow," Colophon said.

"Indeed," said the tour guide. "And this is only one end of Duke Humfrey's Library."

"There's more?"

"Yes. This section was added sometime around 1610. It's called the Arts End."

"Good name," Colophon said.

"I agree," said Ms. Flynn. She pointed to a desk midway up the room to Colophon's left. "Behind the librarian's desk is the original section of Duke Humfrey's Library. It's not part of the tour, but you can go over there and take a look. I suspect you might recognize it."

"Recognize it?" Colophon asked. "How?" She had never been to Oxford.

"It was Hogwarts Library in one of the Harry Potter movies," replied the tour guide.

"Hogwarts Library!"

Ms. Flynn grinned. "Yes. Now hurry and take a quick look. We'll gather back together in a few minutes."

Colophon hurried to the middle of the room and stopped next to the librarian's desk. The librarian glanced up from some papers. Colophon smiled and whispered, "Just looking." The librarian winked at her and then returned her attention to the papers.

The room behind the librarian was magnificent— and Colophon recognized it instantly. Tall dark bookcases protruded from each wall. A wooden desk was built into each bookcase, and chairs were arrayed in front of each desk. On the walls above the bookcases were portraits of men dressed in all manner of ancient garb. Arched wooden beams crossed from one side of the room to the other. And as in the first room, here too the spaces between the beams were filled with row after row of peculiar wooden panels.

Colophon stepped back. Could anything here be a clue? The images painted on the beams? The wooden panels?

Her thoughts were interrupted by the tour guide. "Gather round, everyone!" she called from the large arched window that faced out to the quadrangle.

Colophon rejoined the group.

"We're going to go back downstairs in just a minute to see the Divinity School," Ms. Flynn said. "But first I wanted to show you the building directly across the quadrangle from us." She pointed to a large tower that dominated the far side of the quadrangle. "I mentioned it earlier—it's called the Tower of the Five Orders."

Colophon gasped.

The tower stood five stories tall. Inscribed at the top of the fourth story were two words: BEATI PACIFICI.

CHAPTER TWENTY-FIVE
Denote

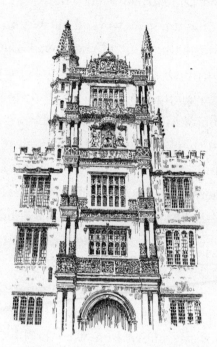

Denote—To serve as a symbol or
name for the meaning of; signify.

Manchester, Georgia
Friday, June 15
8:25 a.m.

The crawlspace was dark and claustrophobic and had an old, musty smell. Case opened his backpack and retrieved a small headlamp flashlight. He secured it to his head and turned it on. There was not enough room to stand up, so he worked his way on hands and knees toward the front of the house. Copper pipes, cast iron drains, and air conditioning ductwork criss-crossed above him. He moved carefully to avoid making any sound. He also knew that all sorts of animals had made their way into this space over the years. Snakes and mice particularly liked the dark, warm environment. The thought of encountering a huge rat snake in the cramped crawlspace did not thrill him. But he continued making his way until he came to a brick wall.

The flashlight on his head illuminated the large brick foundation that supported the front of the house. Directly above him was the library. To his right was a small gray box that connected to the floor above his head. Silver ductwork ran from this box into the dark recesses of the crawlspace. He could hear the slight hum of air being pushed through the ductwork and into the room above. Case reached into his backpack and pulled out a small pocketknife.

✤ ✤ ✤

Bodleian Library
Oxford, England
Friday, June 15
1:25 p.m.

BEATI PACIFICI.

Blessed are the peacemakers.

There it was, directly in front of Colophon, on the building just across the quadrangle: the same Latin inscription that was on the Matriculation Quill at Corpus Christi College.

"Excuse me," Colophon asked Ms. Flynn, "but why is it called the Tower of the Five Orders?"

The tour guide gestured toward the structure. "The tower has five stories, and on each story there are two pairs of columns. Do you see them?"

The group nodded in unison.

"Look at the tops of the columns on each story," she continued. "Notice anything?"

Colophon scanned the tower. "They're different on each story," she said.

"Exactly," replied Ms. Flynn. "The top of the column is called the capital—it's the easiest way to tell them apart. There are five classical orders of columns —Tuscan, Doric, Ionic, Corinthian, and Composite

—each with a unique design. Each order is represented on the tower—hence the name Tower of the Five Orders. The columns were used during various periods in history. For example, if you had traveled to Greece a couple thousand years ago, you would have seen Doric columns all over the place. During the Renaissance, the Composite order was popular."

Ms. Flynn then pointed to a statue sitting just below the window in the quadrangle. "Now the statue below is of William Herbert, the third Earl of . . ."

Colophon didn't hear a thing the tour guide said about the statue. She stared at the tops of the columns on the tower. She had seen the designs before and in the very same pattern—Tuscan, Doric, Ionic, Corinthian, and then Composite.

She edged away from the group. Off to the side, she took out her phone and scrolled through her photos. She stopped at one particular photograph—the Matriculation Quill.

Manchester, Georgia
Friday, June 15
8:40 a.m.

Case made a small incision in the silver tape around one side of the vent box, peeled the tape back, and carefully removed the ductwork. Cool air blew from the ductwork into the crawlspace. Light filtered down through the floor vent directly above him. If he was correct, that floor vent was the one beneath the windows in the library at the front of the house. He removed his iPhone from his backpack, slipped it through one of the slats in the floor vent, and took a photo of the room. The picture was a little fuzzy, but it told him what he needed to know: the room appeared to be unoccupied.

Case reached into his backpack and retrieved a small black cylindrical object. He flipped a switch on the bottom, and a tiny green light flared to life. He listened for signs of movement in the room above but heard nothing. Case pushed up on the vent, which lifted smoothly from the cutout in the floor. With his other hand, he reached up through the hole in the floor and placed the cylindrical object against the baseboard under the window. He then carefully settled the vent back down into place and reattached the air-conditioning duct to the vent box. Cool air once again flowed into the library.

Case returned his pocketknife to his backpack and then crawled back toward the mechanical room.

Chapter Twenty-Six
Dauntless

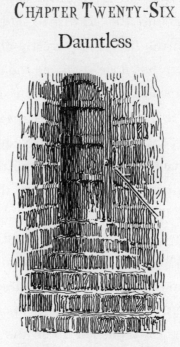

Dauntless — Incapable of being
intimidated or discouraged; fearless.

Bodleian Library
Oxford, England
Friday, June 15
1:40 p.m.

Colophon had to find a way to get to the tower. But
to do so, she had to pass through the reading rooms.
And to enter the reading rooms, she had to find some
excuse to get away from the tour group. And she had

to accomplish all of this before her mom picked her up at the end of the tour.

She glanced over at the tour group. They were still listening to Ms. Flynn discuss the statue in the quadrangle below. No one was paying attention to Colophon. She briefly considered just making a break for the reading rooms. No one would notice—at least not immediately. But it was a small group, and Colophon stood out as the only thirteen-year-old girl. Ms. Flynn or another member of the group would eventually realize she was missing and send someone to look for her.

If she was going to break away from the group, she would have to do it in such a way that everyone knew she had left and why.

Colophon stepped back over to the group just as Ms. Flynn was finishing up her discussion of the statue. "And now," the guide said, "we're going to return downstairs to tour the Divinity School and the rest of the building. But before we go, are there any questions?"

Colophon raised her hand. "Is there a . . . restroom nearby?"

Several members of the group chuckled. Colophon feigned embarrassment. An older gentleman commented under his breath—but loud enough to be heard—that children shouldn't be going on these tours. His wife elbowed him, told him to hush, and then gave Colophon a sympathetic look.

"I'm very sorry," the tour guide said, "but we don't allow guests to use the facilities."

This response generated a groan from the group.

"Oh c'mon," said one man.

"Give the kid a break," said a young American woman.

Anne Flynn sighed. "Very well, vox populi it is. I'll let you into the Lower Reading Room when we head back downstairs. The lavatory is at the far end. Just catch back up with us. The security guard downstairs can direct you."

Colophon nodded. "Thank you. I won't be long—I promise."

Four months ago Meg Letterford's younger sister had approached her about keeping her twin boys for a couple of days while she and her husband attended a wedding in Pittsburgh.

No problem, Meg had eagerly said. We'd love to do it, she insisted.

And then reality had hit home. And when it did, Meg panicked. The twin boys were three months old, and it had been years since she had taken care of an infant—let alone two at the same time. In the days leading up to the visit, she had repeatedly sanitized and resanitized the guest room downstairs. Even though the babies had yet to start crawling, she had baby-proofed everything in the house. She had washed all the linens, towels, and clothes with hypoallergenic laundry detergent. "We can't take any chances," she had repeatedly said to herself and to the rest of the family.

Meg had also purchased a baby monitor. Small, black, and cylindrical, it broadcast a crystal-clear picture and sound. It could be used anywhere in the house—it operated off a battery or could be plugged directly into an electrical socket. Best of all, it streamed its signal directly through the home's Wi-Fi system. All a user had to do was download an app from the manufacturer and voilà, a baby's room could be monitored wirelessly from any smartphone in the house. And monitor she did. Meg's phone had stayed by her side for the entire forty-eight-hour period that she had been responsible for the twins' well-being.

The day after the twins left—and after Meg had slept for fourteen hours straight—Case asked her if he could have the baby monitor.

Colophon protested to their mom, "He's going to use it to spy on me."

Case had denied having any such plan. And truth be told, he had not even thought of using it to spy on his little sister. He just thought it was an extremely cool piece of technology. After his mother gave him a stern warning about respecting his sister's privacy, she had given it to him. He had promptly set the monitor on his shelf and forgotten about it—until two days ago.

Now he sat in the corner of the mechanical room and plugged earbuds into his iPhone. He could watch and listen to everything that occurred in the library—albeit from the perspective of a mouse. But he had only five hours of battery life.

He looked at his watch. It was now 8:50 a.m.

Bodleian Library
Oxford, England
Friday, June 15
1:50 p.m.

Anne Flynn swiped her ID card on the security panel outside the door to the Lower Reading Room. The light on the panel turned green and the door clicked open. Colophon stepped into the reading room. Ms. Flynn reminded her that students might be working and that she should be careful not to disturb anyone.

Then she gave the girl a gentle pat on the shoulder and pulled the door shut. Colophon could hear the tour guide's footsteps on the marble stairway as she descended to the ground floor below.

She glanced at her watch. It was now 1:52 p.m. She had to move quickly.

Colophon walked at a brisk pace through the Lower Reading Room. The difference between the Lower Reading Room and Duke Humfrey's Library was striking. The reading room was filled with row after row of modern reading desks, glittering fluorescent lamps, and comfortable chairs. The bookshelves were lined with volumes that appeared to be of relatively recent vintage. Large windows flooded the room with light. Gone were the ancient books, the dark tones, and the ubiquitous wood paneling of Duke Humfrey's Library. This was not a museum— it was a place for serious study.

A couple of students pored over a book near the middle of the room. They mumbled to each other as Colophon passed but never looked up.

Colophon reached the far end of the room and passed through a narrow doorway into a much smaller room full of equally modern desks and bookshelves. The room branched off to Colophon's left. At the far end of that room was a small set of stone steps leading to an arched wooden door. She glanced through a window to her left. She could see the entrance to the Bodleian Library on the opposite side of the quadrangle. She knew that the room directly above the entrance was Duke Humfrey's Library, and that the Tower of the Five Orders was directly across the quadrangle from the library. If she was right, then the wooden door directly in front of her must lead to the tower.

She made her way quickly across the room and to the top of the steps. She grabbed the ornate brass handle on the door and turned it. The door opened easily. She slipped inside and closed the door behind her.

Manchester, Georgia
Friday, June 15
9:00 a.m.

Treemont was the first person to enter the room. Case watched as he turned on the lights in the library and walked over to a white bulletin board in the middle of the room. When Treemont touched the side of the bulletin board, it flickered and then glowed. This wasn't any ordinary bulletin board, Case realized—

it was a Smart Board, just like the ones they used at school.

Treemont touched the corner of the board. A series of photographs materialized across the top.

He touched one of the photographs, and it expanded until it filled almost the entire board. It was a picture of a long, slender silver object. It appeared to be sitting in a box. Case had no idea what it was.

He tapped the screen on his iPhone and captured a photo of the Smart Board with Treemont standing beside it.

Smile, Case thought.

Tower of the Five Orders
Oxford, England
Friday, June 15
2:00 p.m.

Colophon closed the door behind her and stepped into the tower. The tower room was much larger than it had appeared from the outside. It was lined with bookshelves, and a large wooden table surrounded by chairs sat askew in one corner. The lights were off, and it did not appear as if the room had been used recently. To her left another large window overlooked the quadrangle. In the room's far corner was an open doorway, through which she could see circular stairs leading to the rooms above and the ground floor below. She made her way over to the window and peeked outside. Several tourists milled around in the quadrangle. Across the quadrangle, she could see Duke Humfrey's Library. She knew that she could not chance being seen in the tower, so she dropped to her hands and knees and crawled under the window to the far side of the room.

Colophon stepped into the stairwell and stared up at the narrow circular staircase that spiraled above her. A small rectangular window, high on the thick stone wall, offered a faint light. Even though it was the middle of June, the stairway was cool. A well-worn iron handrail curled around the exterior wall and out of view. Colophon started up the staircase. After several turns she reached a small landing, with a room almost identical to the one she had just left. Based on what Ms. Flynn had told the group, this should be the Upper Reading Room. The next floor up would be the room with the words BEATI PACIFICI carved into the exterior wall.

She continued up the stairs.

CHAPTER TWENTY-SEVEN
Ode

Ode—A lyric poem of some length, usually
of a serious or meditative nature.

Tower of the Five Orders
Oxford, England
Friday, June 15
2:03 p.m.

Dark clouds drifted over the City of Oxford and obscured the afternoon sun. A misty rain started to fall.
What little light had drifted into the tower stairwell
was now gone. Everything was a deep flat gray. The
air was still and cool. Colophon considered whether
she should turn around and rejoin the tour group.
She had, after all, found the next clue. She could

always come back here with Julian. It wasn't as if the tower was going anywhere.

No, she decided. She had to keep going.

Colophon continued up the staircase until she reached the next landing, where she found a narrow wooden door. Above the door was a small hand-painted enamel sign that read ARCHIVES. The door had a large keyhole but no knob or handle. She placed her head against it and listened for any sound from within. She heard nothing.

She leaned against the door and gave it a slight push. It swung open immediately. Losing her balance, she tumbled into the room, hit the floor hard, and rolled over on her side, facing back at the door.

Ouch.

She sat up and rubbed her side.

"Well, that was stupid," she said to no one in particular.

"It happens," a voice behind her said.

Manchester, Georgia
Friday, June 15
9:05 a.m.

Case took a bite of his peanut butter and jelly sandwich. The man and woman he had seen the previous day had just entered the room and were standing next to Treemont. Case recognized the man instantly. It was Brantley Letterford—short, nearly bald, and dressed in a tweed jacket that appeared to be two sizes too big. Brantley nervously cleaned and recleaned his glasses as he stood back and examined the image on the Smart Board. The woman seemed familiar to Case—she was tall and lanky with curly brown hair. He was sure he had seen her at some family function. She held a book in her hand and seemed to be comparing something in it to the image on the screen.

"We've examined this from every angle," Brantley insisted. "We don't even know for certain that it's a clue."

Treemont glared at them. "It's a clue. You'd better have some answers—and soon." He stomped out of the room and slammed the library door behind him.

Brantley stared at the door as if he expected Treemont to reappear at any moment and continue his tirade. He did not. Brantley then retrieved a book from a small side table, sat down, and flipped nervously through the pages. The tall woman stood in front of the Smart Board. With her right index finger, she traced the outline of the silver object on the screen.

Case took another bite of his sandwich. Treemont had said the silver object was a clue. But a clue to what?

This had *Colophon* written all over it.

Tower of the Five Orders
Oxford, England
Friday, June 15
2:05 p.m.

Colophon shot up off the floor in an instant. Standing in the middle of the room next to a tall desk was a middle-aged man with sandy hair. A pair of glasses hung from a chain around his neck. In his hands was a large wooden box. He placed the box on the desk.

"Welcome, Ms. Letterford," the man said in a calm and welcoming tone. "I've been expecting you."

"Excuse me?" She stood and dusted herself off. "You've been expecting me? But how?"

The man walked over to her and offered his hand. "My name is Patrick Addison. I am the Keeper of the Archives for Oxford University."

"The archives?"

"Yes. This floor of the tower has served as the archives for Oxford University for almost four hundred years."

"But why were you expecting me?" she asked. "And how did you know who I am?"

Addison laughed. "Well, as to knowing who you are, you've become quite famous in certain academic circles, haven't you?"

"I suppose," she said. Her parents had tried desperately to keep her out of the spotlight. Even though the discovery of the Shakespeare manuscripts had become world news, Colophon was rarely—if ever —recognized.

"There are a few of us around here who fancy the Bard's work. You're quite the celebrity among us.

"And I might add," he continued, "that my colleagues and I are firmly convinced that the Shakespeare manuscripts are real. Your father is a good man and very well respected."

Emotion welled up in Colophon. How much did Addison know about her family? "He *is* a good man," she finally said. "Thank you for saying that."

"You're quite welcome."

She glanced at her watch. She was running out of time. "Not to be rude, Mr. Addison, but why did you say you were expecting me?"

"A fair question." He pointed up at the ceiling. "I simply assumed that you would eventually find your way here to look at that."

Colophon looked up. The ceiling was made up of small wooden panels—identical in size and shape to the panels on the ceiling in Duke Humfrey's Library. They were all painted in a dazzling royal blue and were separated from one another by thick wooden beams. A word was printed in gold on each panel. Colophon moved to the center of the room and turned around until she could read the panels in proper order.

To His excellency James King
of Great Britain ys sixteen

day of ye tenth month
in ye year of ovr

lord MDCXXII ys room be
dedicated. Thovgh ye oxen plow

and ye earth wrovght its
noble bovnty, tis thy embrace

os knowledge that doth permit
ye flovrishing of this fertile

soil north of ye Thames.
Along its banks ye river

HATH ENGRAVED UPON YS LAND

YE FLEET BEQVEST OF THOV

EXCELLENCY'S GREAT MERCIES. SVCH

BE YE SIGN OF THY REGENCY

THAT YS CHAMBER HATH PERMITTED

GREAT ENDEAVORS. THVS SHALL THY

HVMBLE SERVANT HEREBY LEAVE HIS

MARK THIS DAY. MILES LETTERFORD

"Miles Letterford!" Colophon exclaimed.

Addison seemed surprised by her reaction. "Why, of course. I assumed you knew that your ancestor donated the funds for the furnishing of this room."

He pointed to the large, ornate wooden shelves that lined each wall and reached almost to the ceiling. Tall ladders attached to brass railings that ran across the walls provided access to the upper shelves. "Everything in the room was paid for by Miles Letterford. He was apparently quite generous in his donation."

"And the statue on the outside?" asked Colophon. "The one that says 'Beati pacifici'?"

"Miles Letterford's contribution as well," he said. "It was King James's royal motto."

She stared at the ceiling. "Is there anything . . . strange about the dedication?"

"The dedication? No, nothing particularly strange. I suspect that you'd find similar dedications throughout England. But there is something else that I discovered—something that lends a slightly different perspective to this particular dedication."

Addison moved to the center of the room and gestured for Colophon to do the same.

"Do you see the wooden panels that run around the room, just below the ceiling?"

Colophon nodded. They were hard to miss—the four carved wooden panels were magnificent, one just below the ceiling on each wall. Carved into each panel was a tree. The branches and leaves of each tree unfurled along the walls and just below the ceiling.

"There's a different tree carved on each wall—oak, maple, ash, and yew. I've looked at those panels for years and years and thought nothing of them. Mere decoration, I assumed."

"They're not?"

"I don't believe so," he replied. "I think there's

something else." He pointed to a portion of a panel in the far corner. It was an image of an acorn. "What do you see?"

"An acorn," she said.

"Exactly." He rolled one of the ladders to the far corner. "Please take a closer look."

She climbed up the ladder until she was only a few feet from the carving of the acorn. The detail was incredible, but what was Addison talking about?

And then she saw it. Carved into the detail of the acorn cap was the letter X.

She looked down at him. "It's the letter X."

"No," he replied, "it's the number ten—in Roman numerals. I noticed that very carving three years ago as I was returning a box to the upper shelf. And I noticed something else. Look at the rest of the tree."

She looked a couple of feet to her right. It took a second, but she found it. Carved into an oak leaf and hidden among the leaf's veins was the Roman numeral V. Farther down she spied the Roman numeral III hidden in a branch of the tree.

"It continues down the entire wall—all hidden within the leaves, branches, trunk, and acorns of the oak tree," Addison said.

Colophon scanned the length of the panel. The

Roman numerals now jumped out at her. She also noticed that they were not in numerical order. "But what do they mean?"

"There's more. Look at the maple tree running across the wall to your left."

She turned and looked at a large maple leaf carved into the panel near the corner of the wall.

"The letter A?" she said. "Is that the letter A carved into the leaf?"

"Of a sorts," Addison said, smiling. "Keep looking."

She looked a couple of feet down the panel and identified the letter B in the branch of the maple tree.

"It's the letter B," she said.

"Keep looking."

She stretched out as far as she could to get a closer look at a large maple leaf farther down the panel. There was clearly something carved into it, but she was confused. "Is that . . . an upside-down L?" she asked. "And isn't it backwards?"

Addison clapped his hands together in delight. "Excellent! It's actually the Greek letter gamma— which looks like an upside-down and backwards L."

"So that isn't an A and B in the first two carvings?"

"No," replied Addison. "Those are the Greek letters alpha and beta. And the carvings continue down the length of the panel—alpha, beta, gamma, delta, epsilon, zeta, eta, theta, iota, and kappa. The first ten letters in the Greek alphabet—all hidden within the leaves and branches of the maple tree."

Colophon stepped down from the ladder. "Are those coordinates?" She had learned in math class that coordinates could be used to identify a specific point on a flat surface. But coordinates usually came in pairs.

"Close," replied Addison. "There are exactly one hundred panels on the ceiling—ten across and ten down. There are ten Roman numerals and ten Greek letters. Each word in the dedication corresponds to a specific set of coordinates—a Greek letter and a Roman numeral. I am convinced that there's a message hidden somewhere within the dedication."

A message!

Colophon could barely contain herself. "So what is the message? Have you deciphered it?"

He sat down in a chair near the desk and sighed. "I'm afraid that has escaped me. Without knowing the specific coordinates I'm looking for, I'd simply be guessing."

But Colophon did not have to guess. She knew in a flash exactly where the coordinates could be found.

She pulled out her phone. "Do you mind if I take a photo of the ceiling?"

"By all means." He then scribbled down the sequence of Roman numerals and Greek letters on the back of one of his business cards and handed it to Colophon. "You won't be able to see the letters and numbers in a photograph," he said, "but this should help. And please do me the favor of letting me know if you ever decipher the code."

Colophon grinned. "You bet. But I'd better be going —I broke off from the tour group, and they're probably looking for me by now. I don't think I'm supposed to be up here."

"Our secret," he replied. "And good luck."

Colophon thanked Mr. Addison for his help and stepped into the stairwell. The door closed behind her. She immediately pulled out her phone and texted the photo of the ceiling to Julian. "Next clue attached. We have work to do," she typed.

Colophon stuffed the phone back into her pocket and hurried down the stairs to catch up with the group.

Chapter Twenty-Eight
Eyeball

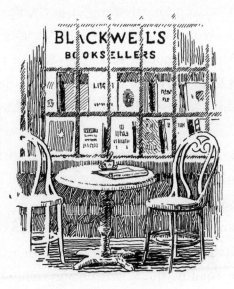

Eyeball—The eye itself.

Blackwell's Booksellers
Broad Street
Oxford, England
Friday, June 15
2:15 p.m.

Trigue James sat in the bookstore's café, sipped on his latte, and thumbed through a magazine. It had been a relatively boring day, but he wasn't complaining. Young Ms. Letterford had yet to send or receive a text or an e-mail, and there had been no phone calls. In fact, James was not even convinced that the girl was looking for anything in particular. She had not been accompanied by her usual sidekick, and he didn't think her mother was involved. But he was being paid to monitor her every move—so here he sat sipping his latte, which was just fine by him.

Ping.

James looked down at his phone. The girl had just sent a text.

He opened it.

The words *next clue* were all he needed to see.

He forwarded the message to Treemont, then returned to reading the magazine and sipping his latte.

Manchester, Georgia
Friday, June 15
9:16 a.m.

Something was going on. Brantley Letterford and the woman had left the library with Treemont a few minutes ago. When they returned, they were obviously excited about something. Treemont walked up to the Smart Board. He touched the corner of the screen and a new image appeared. It was a series of blue squares separated by brown lines.

"Remarkable," said the tall woman.

"I would never have guessed," said Brantley. "And a thirteen-year-old girl no less."

Coly!

Case was now officially worried.

Treemont seemed more agitated than ever. "We now have the advantage. I don't expect to lose it. There is obviously a message hidden in those squares."

"For goodness' sake, Treemont, we're not experts in cryptology," said the tall woman. Her tone was cool and calm. She did not seem the least bit intimidated by him. "And without a key of some sort, it will be nearly impossible."

"We would simply be guessing," pleaded Brantley.

Treemont turned and faced them. "Then either guess well or find the key—but be quick about it. I leave for London this evening."

Case tapped the screen on his phone and captured a photo of Treemont and the others looking at the blue squares. It was time to contact Colophon. Whatever was happening was happening fast. He attached the two photos to a text to Colophon: "I'm in the house watching Trecmont. He's up to something. Look at the photos." He hit send and then returned to watching Brantley argue with the woman. Brantley seemed in genuine anguish over the image on the screen.

Blackwell's Booksellers
Broad Street
Oxford, England
Friday, June 15
2:17 p.m.

Ping.

James looked down at his phone. The girl had now received a text—apparently from her brother. Things were heating up.

He opened the message, looked at the attached photos, and smiled.

These kids were impressive. He was almost tempted to delete the message and see what happened.

But business was business.

He forwarded the text to Treemont, but not before adding a small message of his own.

✦ ✦ ✦

Manchester, Georgia
Friday, June 15
9:18 a.m.

Ping.

Treemont looked down at his phone. Another message from Trigue James. He stepped into the hallway, closed the door, and opened it.

"Nice tie," the message read.

Treemont scrolled down and looked at the attachments: photos of himself—one taken no more than two or three minutes ago—from within the library.

Bodleian Library
Oxford, England
Friday, June 15
2:18 p.m.

Colophon had located the tour group standing in a corner of the quadrangle. She made her apologies to Ms. Flynn, then stood quietly to the side as the guide discussed the history of the quadrangle's construction.

Ping.

Colophon pulled her phone from her pocket. It was

a text from Case. She took one look at it and gasped. The group turned and looked at her.

"Excuse me," said Ms. Flynn, "but are you okay?"

Colophon's face had turned white. She felt as if she had been punched in the stomach. She had to get away from the group and think. "I need to sit down."

"Why don't you go back into the entrance hall and have a seat?" said Ms. Flynn. "It's nice and cool in there."

Colophon nodded and headed inside. She found a bench near the security desk.

It can't be, she thought. *Maybe I was mistaken.*

She opened Case's text once again and looked at the photos.

She had not been mistaken.

Case had just sent her two photos. One of them showed Treemont standing in front of the image of the Matriculation Quill that she had taken at Corpus Christi College. But the second photograph upset her even more. It was a picture of Treemont standing in front of a photo she had taken mere minutes ago in the Tower of the Five Orders.

How was that possible?

Immediately she realized—someone was monitoring her phone. And whoever was monitoring her phone also knew that Case was in the house. And that meant Treemont knew.

Colophon's stomach churned. She had to warn Case, but how?

Chapter Twenty-Nine
Excitements

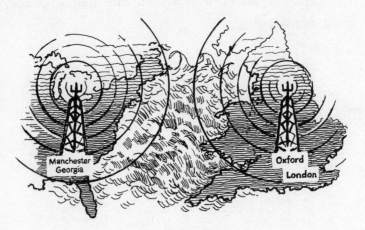

Excitements—Things that excite.

Manchester, Georgia
Friday, June 15
9:20 a.m.

Case had watched Treemont leave the room after receiving what appeared to be a text. He returned a few seconds later and asked Brantley and the woman to leave. He shut the library door behind them. He pulled a chair from the side of the room and placed it directly in front of the Smart Board, facing the camera. He then brought over a small side table and placed it next to the chair. He stepped out of view for a second and returned with a cup of coffee, which he placed on the side table.

What's he up to?

Treemont sat down in the chair, took a sip of the coffee, and stared directly at the camera.

"Good morning, Case," Treemont said.

Case could hear feet pounding above him throughout the house.

They were searching for him.

The Bodleian Library
Oxford, England
Friday, June 15
2:20 p.m.

Colophon stared at her phone. If she contacted Case, whoever was monitoring her phone would know immediately what she was doing. But she had no choice. She had to warn him and hope that he had time to get out of the house.

Her message was short and to the point: "They are spying on my phone. Get out. Now."

✦ ✦ ✦

Manchester, Georgia
Friday, June 15
9:21 a.m.

Case's phone vibrated. It was a text from his sister. He read the message and then flipped back to watching Treemont, who continued to sit calmly in the library sipping a cup of coffee.

Case had to find a way out of the house. It was only a matter of time before they would discover him.

The footsteps continued to pound above him. He could also hear voices outside the house. And then he heard footsteps in the basement. They were headed toward the mechanical room.

He looked around the room. There was nowhere else to hide.

The footsteps were getting closer. And then there was silence.

Were they going back upstairs?

Suddenly the doorknob to the mechanical room shook violently. The noise caught Case off guard. His heart beat furiously.

"Does anyone have a key to this room?" a man yelled.

"Kick the door in!" another man yelled. "Treemont won't care."

Case considered making a break for the window and taking his chances in the open. But he could now hear voices just outside the window too.

He had only one chance, he realized. He pulled out his phone and pecked out a quick text to Colophon. He then sat back and hoped it would work.

The Bodleian Library
Oxford, England
Friday, June 15
2:22 p.m.

Ping.

Colophon looked down at her phone. The text from Case read: "Everything's OK. I'm in the tree-house."

Broad Street
Oxford, England
Friday, June 15
2:22 p.m.

Ping.

Trigue James looked at his phone. It was a text to the girl from her older brother.

He read it as he walked down Broad Street toward

the train station. He stopped and dutifully forwarded the message to Treemont.

It was, after all, his job.

He placed his phone back in his coat pocket.

Clever kid, he thought. *Very clever.*

Manchester, Georgia
Friday, June 15
9:23 a.m.

Ping.

Treemont looked down at the text from Trigue James.

Treehouse? he wondered. *What treehouse?*

He left the library and went outside. He found one of the security guards standing by the side of the house.

"Do you know anything about a treehouse?" he demanded.

"Yes, sir," the guard replied. "We found it yesterday. It's on the far side of the pasture hidden in the trees."

"That's where the boy is hiding," said Treemont.

BAM!

Case cringed as someone kicked the door. The me-

chanical room had a fireproof metal door and frame
—but they wouldn't hold up forever.

BAM!

He heard the locking mechanism crack. One more
good kick and it would burst open.

He waited for the next blow.

But it never came.

The next thing he heard was footsteps going up
the stairs from the basement, then beating across
the floor toward the front of the house. He heard the
front door slam shut. The voice outside the window
was also gone.

He grabbed his backpack and slung it over his
shoulder, made his way over to the window, and
peeked outside. All clear. He opened the window and
pulled himself up and onto the lawn. No one was
around. He sprinted for the woods, then ran until he
reached the far side of the property, where he col-
lapsed beside a large pine tree. He gasped for air. His
sides ached. His head pounded. But he was safe.

What would Treemont say when he realized the
treehouse was empty? Case would have paid anything to see the look on his face.

Case started to laugh, but then it hit him.

He was safe, but Colophon was not.

Someone had been spying on Colophon. Whatever

Colophon was looking for, Treemont seemed convinced that she was close.

Case needed to talk to his sister.

The Bodleian Library
Oxford, England
Friday, June 15
3:01 p.m.

Colophon paced anxiously at the entrance to the Bodleian Library. She had no idea if Case was safe, or if . . .

She didn't want to think about the alternative.

She spied her mother walking across the quadrangle and sprinted to her. She had no choice but to tell her what was happening. Maybe she could call the police. Maybe she could do something to help Case.

"Mom!" she yelled. "It's Case! We have to—"

But before she could finish her sentence, Meg Letterford thrust her phone at Colophon. "I know it's Case," she said. "It's for you."

Colophon took the phone and stared at it. How did her mother know? Was it the police? Had something already happened to Case? A million different horrible scenarios raced through her mind as Colophon held the phone to her ear and said, "Hello."

"Afternoon, dorkette," Case said. "Were you worried about your big brother?"

"Case!" She glanced at her mother, who eyed her suspiciously.

"I'm okay," he said. "But it was close there for a moment."

"But how . . . you said you were in the treehouse?"

"Never went there."

She realized what had happened. Of course he hadn't gone to the treehouse. "That was. . . . brilliant," she said. "But you're still a jerk. I was worried."

"Listen, you need to be careful. I'm not exactly sure what Treemont's looking for, but he's convinced you've found some sort of clue."

"I have," she said. She knew there was a message hidden in the ceiling of the archives room. All she needed was more time to decipher it.

"Don't do anything stupid," Case said. "Since someone was tapping your phone, they may also be following you. I'm flying to London tomorrow with Aunt Audrey. I'll be there late in the afternoon."

"I'm glad you're safe, Case."

"Don't do anything stupid," he repeated.

Chapter Thirty
Engagements

Engagements — Promises or agreements to be
at a particular place at a particular time.

Paddington Station
London, England
Friday, June 15
5:03 p.m.

"This train terminates at Paddington Station," a
voice announced over the intercom as the train eased
to a stop. Colophon and her mother gathered their
belongings and moved toward the exit.

The doors popped open, and the large crowd of
people returning from Oxford streamed onto the

platform and toward the exit. Colophon grabbed her mother's arm and held tight as they made their way through the crowd.

"Coly!" a voice yelled.

She looked around.

"Coly!" the voice yelled again.

It was her father.

Mull Letterford stood by the exit waving his arms in the air. Maggie sat by his side on a leash. Her whole body wagged excitedly. Colophon rushed over and gave Maggie a hug.

"So only the dog gets a hug?" said her father. "I suppose she walked herself all the way over to the station to meet you."

Colophon stood up and hugged her father. "I'm glad to see you too!"

Meg Letterford gave her husband a kiss on the cheek. "This is a nice surprise."

"Such a beautiful day," said Mull, "and the dog insisted."

Colophon took Maggie's leash as they headed for the exit. "How was work today?" she asked her father.

"Well, let's see. One of our reporters was out sick, so I had the pleasure of interviewing a cat named Ms. Tootsy, who was apparently abducted by aliens while her family was on holiday at Cornwall."

"A cat?"

"Named Ms. Tootsy," replied Mull. "And did I mention she had been abducted by aliens?"

Colophon watched her father take her mother's hand as they walked.

He deserves better than this, Colophon thought. It didn't matter if Treemont kept the company and the house in Manchester. But the truth did matter. Her father wasn't a liar, a fraud, or a cheat. The manuscripts were real. Marlowe or Shakespeare—it really didn't matter who wrote them. Her father was a good man, and finding the real treasure—or whatever might be at the end of this search—would prove that.

Colophon pulled out her phone and sent a text to Julian: "Can you be at the house tomorrow? Reply yes or no only. Don't send any other messages. I'll explain later."

Seconds later her phone pinged. It was a text from Julian that read simply: "Yes."

Trigue James watched as the girl, her parents, and the dog left the train station in the direction of Clerkenwell, the neighborhood of the Letterford residence. If they intended to walk to Clerkenwell, he could easily beat them there in a cab. He had parked a van across the street from their home several days ago. It had served as his base of operations ever since.

Treemont had been very specific in his last instructions before departing for England.

"Don't lose sight of them," he had insisted.

But James knew how to do his job and knew that it would be too much of a risk to follow them on foot, particularly since they had a dog in tow. His best bet was to get to the house ahead of them and prepare. Whatever was happening, Treemont expected it to happen soon. James was concerned that Treemont was pushing too fast, too hard. He was becoming anxious—and James didn't like anxious. Anxious people went to prison, and that was one place James never intended to set foot.

But a job was a job. And he would do his job.

Letterford residence
Clerkenwell, London, England
Saturday, June 16
10:33 a.m.

Julian sipped his coffee as he examined the photograph of the ceiling from the Tower of the Five Orders. Colophon had explained to him that the Keeper of the Archives was convinced that a message was hidden in the dedication.

Julian agreed.

Colophon then explained that Treemont had obtained a copy of the photograph just minutes after she had taken it, and that someone was clearly monitoring her phone.

That meant, Julian noted, that Treemont knew everything they knew.

"Almost everything," Colophon said.

She handed him the card that the Keeper of the Archives had given her.

"Treemont doesn't have this," she said. Then she told Julian about the Roman numerals and Greek letters inscribed in the paneling in the archive room.

Julian examined the Roman numerals and Greek letters on the card. "Clever," he said. "The Roman numerals aren't in numeric order. So even if someone had a set of coordinates, they would still need to know the order of the numerals. But that brings us to another problem—we don't have the coordinates."

Colophon smiled. "But we do."

She pulled four photographs from a folder and placed them on the table. Julian immediately recognized them as the sides of the silver presentation box in which the Matriculation Quill had been stored. Each photograph showed four sets of symbols—one from each side of the box.

AVIII	ZII	ΓVIII	ZV
ZIII	KIX	ZVIII	KIV
ΓII	ZVII	HI	IVIII
KV	ZIX	KVII	ZIV

"See," Colophon said. "A Greek letter followed by a Roman numeral. I knew it as soon as I saw the paneling."

"Remarkable," Julian replied. "We have the coordinates! Have you deciphered the answer yet?"

She sighed. "I tried. I mean, it was easy enough to get the words from the dedication. I'm just not sure what sequence to put them in. The sides of the box weren't numbered."

Julian looked at the photograph of the ceiling. "What if they're already in the correct order?"

"But what order is that?"

"The order in the dedication." He took the photograph of the ceiling and wrote the Roman numerals across the top of the photo just as they were positioned on the panels. He then wrote the Greek letters down the side of the photo. Ten Roman numerals across—ten Greek letters down. "Now we just have to match them up with the words in the dedication," he said. "Give me a set of coordinates from the box."

"Alpha and Roman numeral eight," she read.

He found the Greek letter alpha down the side of the photograph and placed his left index finger on it. He then found the Roman numeral eight on the top of the photograph and placed his right index finger on it. Slowly he moved his right finger down and his left finger across the dedication until his fingers met at the word *sixteen*. He circled the word.

"Next set of coordinates?" he asked.

"Zeta and Roman numeral two," said Colophon.

In a similar manner, he located and then circled the word *ye*.

Colophon continued, "Gamma and Roman numeral eight."

Julian located and circled the word *plow*.

"Zeta and Roman numeral five."

Julian located and circled the word *north*.

They continued through the entire list with Julian circling each word on the photograph as Colophon read off the coordinates. When they reached the final set, Julian picked up the photograph. "Write this down," he said to Colophon. "'Sixteen oxen plow north of ye Thames along ye river fleet thy servant leave his mark.'"

Colophon looked confused. "That doesn't make much sense."

"Let's see if we can clear it up a bit," Julian said. "First, let's change the word 'ye' to 'the.' It means the same thing."

Colophon made the changes.

It now read: *Sixteen oxen plow north of the Thames along the river fleet thy servant leave his mark.*

"Still doesn't make much sense," she said.

"Patience," he replied. "Let's assume that there are different phrases, and it's not one long confusing sentence."

"That's reasonable, I suppose."

"Okay," he said, "so the phrase 'north of the Thames' is clearly a direction of some sort."

"The River Thames?" she said. "The one that runs through London?"

"Correct," he replied.

"All right, so at least one phrase makes sense. But what does 'sixteen oxen plow' mean?"

Julian stared at the photograph. "I hate to suggest this," he said. "It goes against everything I believe. But why don't you Google it?"

Colophon flipped open her laptop. "Finally, you see the light."

She typed in the phrase "sixteen oxen plow."

"How many results?" he asked.

"Almost two million," she replied.

"Ouch," he said. "Well, it looks like we are going to have to—"

"Wait," she interrupted. "One of the first results is an encyclopedia entry for the word *furlong*. It says that a furlong was the distance a pair of oxen could plow without resting."

"So sixteen oxen—or eight pairs of oxen," he noted, "could plow eight furlongs."

"And according to this entry," she continued, "a furlong is equal to forty rods—whatever that means—or one-eighth of a mile."

"So eight furlongs would be—"

"A mile!" she exclaimed.

"Let's try this again," he said. "A mile north of the River Thames, along the river fleet, thy servant leave his mark."

"We're getting closer," said Colophon. "I'm guessing 'servant' refers to Miles Letterford and his 'mark' would be the symbol for the Greek letter sigma."

"Clever work!" said Julian. "So that leaves one phrase—'along the river fleet.'"

"Maybe it's referring to a river named Fleet. Is that possible?"

Julian sat down. "That's entirely possible. The Fleet River was a prominent landmark in London during Miles's time."

"So we've solved the hidden message!" Colophon said excitedly. "A mile north of the River Thames, along the Fleet River, Miles Letterford left his mark."

"Except for one small detail," Julian said. "The Fleet River no longer exists."

Chapter Thirty-One

Negotiate

Negotiate—To confer with another in order
to come to terms or reach an agreement.

Letterford residence
Clerkenwell, London, England
Saturday, June 16
11:00 a.m.

"What do you mean, it no longer exists?" asked Colophon. "How does a river just disappear?"

"It didn't disappear," Julian replied. "It was covered up. The river used to be a fairly substantial waterway that flowed into the Thames. But then as London grew, it started being used more and more as a sewer."

"Eww," she said.

"Well, London in the sixteenth and seventeenth centuries was not exactly known for its pleasant smells and sanitation. But even by those standards, the Fleet River was considered bad. The river was converted into a canal, and then the canal was covered up because of the stench."

"So the river's gone?"

"Not exactly," he replied. "It's still there—but it's now underground. In the middle of the nineteenth century, it was incorporated into London's sewer system."

"An underground river?"

"Yes, I suppose so. And did I mention it's part of the sewer system?"

"Still, an underground river is pretty cool," she said. "So all we have to do is find the entrance to the underground river and head north for a mile."

Julian sighed. "I was afraid you'd feel that way. Our last experience with an underground river does not make me eager to give it another try."

"C'mon, it wasn't that bad," Colophon said. Their

adventure in Stratford-upon-Avon may have been treacherous, but it had also provided an important clue. "And what choice do we have? This may be the final clue—the clue you've been looking for your entire life. And we know that Treemont is looking for it too. Even if Treemont doesn't have the information from the paneling in the tower, what if Miles Letterford left other clues—clues we haven't uncovered? Isn't that possible?"

Julian nodded. He thought of the book he had found in Wales. It was quite possible—perhaps probable—that Miles Letterford had left other clues—other paths to the same end.

"So what if Treemont gets there first?" she asked. "Could you live with that?"

Julian leaned back in his chair and closed his eyes. "I've put you in enough danger already," he finally responded. "I can't do it again."

"Then I'll do it without you," she insisted. They had followed the clues from the inkwell to the quill to the dedication in the Tower of the Five Orders. She couldn't stop now. "You can either help me or get out of my way. It's your choice."

Colophon stood up. "Treemont trashed my father's name and stole his business. I have to do this!"

Julian sat up in his chair and stared across the table at her. He had come to recognize that determined look in her eyes.

"I have one condition," he said finally. "We have to let someone know what we're doing. If anything happens down there, *someone* needs to know where we are."

She started to object, but he interrupted her. "We have to. This isn't a game."

She considered what he had said and knew he was right. Someone had to know what was going on. "Case and Aunt Audrey will be here after lunch," she said. "Mom's in Oxford for the day, and Dad's at work. I'll call my dad and let him know that we're going out for a bit, and then I'll leave a note for Case that explains everything. By the time Case gets here, we'll be back home. This'll be easy—you'll see."

The note was simple and straightforward:

> Case:.
>   Julian and I have discovered the next clue. It
> is located a mile up the Fleet River. The Fleet
> River is part of London's sewer system and is
> underground. The entrance to the river is below

> Blackfriars Bridge on the Thames. It is perfectly
> safe, so don't worry. We are leaving immediately.
>
> Colophon

She scribbled the time—11:55 a.m.—on the bottom of the note and placed it in an envelope. Then she wrote Case's name on the outside of the envelope and set it on his bed. Julian was waiting for her at the bottom of the stairs when she finished. He had a worried look on his face.

"This could be dangerous," he said. "There are more than thirteen thousand miles of sewer lines below London. There's no cell service and no one to stop and ask for directions. If we get lost, it could be days —weeks—before anyone finds us."

"We won't get lost," she assured him. "We'll head straight up the river, find what we're looking for, and head straight back."

"Straight in and straight out. Nothing more?"

"Nothing more," she repeated. "I promise."

Trigue James watched the girl and her cousin step outside the Letterford home and make their way down to the sidewalk. The fact that they both had bags slung over their shoulders did not escape his notice. He sent a text to Treemont: "Something is happening. Be ready."

A few moments later a cab pulled up in front of the Letterford residence, and the girl and her cousin climbed inside. James waited until the cab was half-way down the block before following it.

Chapter Thirty-Two
Stealthy

Stealthy — Marked by or acting with quiet,
caution, and secrecy intended to avoid notice.

Blackfriars Bridge
London, England
Saturday, June 16
12:30 p.m.

The taxi pulled over to the side of the roadway at the
north end of Blackfriars Bridge. The traffic on the
bridge was heavy, so Colophon and Julian quickly
pulled their bags from the seat and exited to the

sidewalk. The taxi sped away and was swallowed by the mass of cars heading south.

"The entrance to the Fleet River is directly below this end of the bridge," Julian said as he threw his bag over his shoulder and started for a set of stairs at the side of the bridge.

Colophon put on her backpack and hurried after him. "How do you know so much about the Fleet River?" she asked as they descended.

He laughed. "Honestly, are you really surprised that I would know about a mysterious river hidden for hundreds of years below London?"

She paused. Julian knew every obscure fact that there was to know about anything that could have any impact on his search for the Letterford treasure. And facts about Miles Letterford's hometown—London—were particularly relevant to that endeavor.

"No," she finally replied. "I'm not surprised."

The traffic thundered above them as Colophon and Julian wound their way down the stairs to a path that ran under the bridge and along the Thames. They stepped into the deep shadows cast by the bridge and over to the black iron railing that separated the path from the river below. They stared over the railing at the Thames.

"Do you see the bubbles and the frothing water directly below us?" Julian asked.

Colophon nodded. "It seems to be coming from the bank of the river."

"Exactly. That's where the Fleet flows into the Thames," he said. "We can enter there and head north."

"That's a long way down." She was looking at the swirling waters below.

Julian pointed to a narrow set of iron stairs that led to the embankment below. An iron gate in front of the stairs read AUTHORIZED PERSONNEL ONLY. Colophon tried the knob, and it turned easily.

"I guess they aren't worried about people wanting to get into the sewers," she said.

Julian casually opened the gate just wide enough for them to squeeze through. "When I say 'Go,' follow me as quickly as you can. And don't look back. We need to make it inside the entrance to the sewer before anyone spots us."

Julian waited until a young couple strolling on the walkway passed them, then whispered "Go," slipped inside the gate, and clambered down the iron stairs. Colophon stepped inside the gate, carefully pulled it shut, and scampered down behind him. Within seconds, they were inside the entrance to the sewer and outside the view of the rest of the world.

Colophon looked down the passageway. It was constructed of a deep red brick. A small ledge ran down the length of the passageway and into the darkness. The gurgling of water and other strange sounds echoed down the long chamber. And it was cool—almost cold—inside the entrance.

"Welcome to the Fleet River," Julian said.

Trigue James cursed himself for being caught off guard. He had not expected the taxi to stop on the bridge. From several car lengths back, he watched the girl and her cousin get out of the taxi and head down a set of stairs at the side of the bridge. Looking down, he saw a walkway running beneath the bridge and along the Thames. If they made it to the path before he could get down there, he would almost certainly lose them.

But he didn't have time to backtrack and find a parking space.

James looked around. There were no police cars in sight. He would have to take a chance—something he didn't like to do. He pulled the van up onto the sidewalk, jumped out, and rushed to the stairs. At the first landing he stopped and looked down at the walkway. The girl and her cousin were still there. They were standing by the railing at the side of the river. He moved back up the stairs to be out of their line of sight.

James peeked around the corner. They were now standing by an access gate at the edge of the walkway. It led to a set of iron stairs running down the side of the embankment to the river below. The girl's cousin scanned the walkway—James snapped his head back to avoid being seen. He paused for a moment, then looked back around the corner just in time to see the girl descending the stairs. At the bottom she vanished into the embankment.

James fired off a text to Treemont: "Meet me at north end of Blackfriars Bridge—immediately." James put the phone away and hurried back to his van to find a place to park. He knew he needed to hurry—Treemont would be there soon.

Case was exhausted.

He had not slept a wink on the entire flight from Atlanta. The large man in the seat next to him had sneezed, hacked, and coughed for eight straight hours. But that wasn't the only reason Case couldn't fall asleep. Colophon had been right all along—

Treemont was at the center of everything. And now there were even more questions. How was Brantley involved? And the tall woman in the library? Was there anyone else?

Treemont had destroyed his father's reputation and stolen his company. But recently Case had also become convinced of something else: Treemont was dangerous. He wasn't going to let anything or anyone stand in his way. And that worried Case.

He trudged up the stairs and threw his duffel bag into the corner of his room. His sister was not at home, so he sent her a text: "Call me—I'm home."

Case yawned deeply. He needed to talk to his sister. It was time for Colophon to tell their parents what was going on.

He checked his messages. Colophon had not yet responded.

He dialed her number. No answer.

She's probably with Mom—or Dad.

Case yawned again.

A short nap won't hurt.

CHAPTER THIRTY-THREE
Forward

Forward—Ardently inclined; eager.

Fleet River
London, England
Saturday, June 16
12:45 p.m.

Julian handed Colophon a flashlight.

"Be careful," he said. "I've heard tales of things that live down here."

"Things?" she asked. "What things?"

"The usual. Rats, white crabs, scorpions."

She made a mental note to watch where she stepped.

Julian shined his flashlight down the tunnel. "Pirate ships once sailed this river," he said.

"Pirate ships? How could anything have sailed on this?"

"Hard to believe, isn't it?" he said. "But the Fleet was once wide and deep. Barges, boats, and yes, pirate ships once sailed its waters."

Julian stepped up on the brick ledge that ran along the length of the wall. He extended his hand to Colophon and pulled her up.

"We've got a long way to go," he said. "We'd best start." He pointed his flashlight into the darkness and started walking.

Colophon followed quickly. "How will we know when we've traveled a mile? I doubt they have signposts."

Julian pulled a small round object from his belt and showed it to her. "A pedometer."

She recognized it instantly. Her mother used a pedometer when she took her evening walk to let her know how far she had gone.

"It's not entirely precise." He clipped it back on his belt. "But it should get us close enough."

Colophon paused. There was a question she needed to ask, but she was afraid of the answer. "How do we know the mark is even still down here? It seems like there have been a lot of changes to the river since Miles Letterford was around."

"True," Julian said. "But some parts of the river haven't changed. Segments were bricked and covered for centuries before the river became part of a centralized sewer system. One of those areas is not far from your home in London."

"Near my home?"

"Yes. What's the name of your neighborhood?"

"Clerkenwell," she said. "What does that have to do with the river?"

"Clerkenwell is a very old area of London," he said. "And did you know that it was named after a well that was used to provide water to the surrounding homes? The well was known as the Clerk's Well —that's how the neighborhood became known as Clerkenwell. The well was hidden for many, many years but was recently rediscovered. Apparently it had been covered up when it became too polluted— just like the river next to it."

Colophon smiled. "The Fleet River."

"Exactly."

"So there's a chance that whatever Miles left is still down here?"

He nodded. "The well is still there, so maybe whatever Miles left behind still exists."

"And what do you think he left behind?" she asked. "Something that proves the manuscripts are real? Something that'll prove my father's not a liar?"

The sounds of the Thames River faded into the distance as they walked. "I don't know," Julian finally replied. "As I said, there's always a chance."

Blackfriars Bridge
London, England
Saturday, June 16
1:00 p.m.

James stood next to the railing of Blackfriars Bridge and stared down at the Thames River flowing beneath him. A tall man in a dark suit walked over and stood beside him.

"You're not exactly dressed for the occasion, are you?" James said.

"You didn't tell me what the occasion was," Treemont replied. James noted a testiness in Treemont's voice and demeanor.

"No," said James, "I suppose I didn't. Then again, the girl and her cousin didn't exactly share their itinerary with me."

He proceeded toward the stairs at the north end of the bridge. "Follow me."

Treemont growled under his breath and followed.

James descended the stairs and stepped over to the exact point under the bridge where he had seen Colophon and Julian standing. He gestured to the access gate and the iron stairs leading down to the embankment. "They disappeared into the embankment. Some sort of sewer line, I suppose. You'll need to go down the stairs to follow them."

"You're not joining me?" Treemont asked.

James handed him his flashlight. "Sewers are not my cup of tea. I've done my job. It's now up to you."

Treemont tested the weight and balance of the heavy metal flashlight in his right hand. "Fine," he replied. "Then it's up to me to finish this."

James smiled. "Be careful. The little girl's quite clever."

Treemont scowled, then turned and headed down the iron stairs.

James watched him disappear into the embankment. He then removed his cell phone from his coat pocket, checked to make sure no one was watching, and dropped it into the flowing current of the Thames.

He would leave the van parked where it was. It didn't matter—it had been rented under a false

name and had been wiped down to remove any fin-
gerprints. He had a car parked in a garage near Victoria Station. With any luck he would reach the Manchester Airport by early evening. From there, who
knew?

Chapter Thirty-Four
Premeditated

Premeditate — Characterized by deliberate
purpose, previous consideration,
and some degree of planning.

**Fleet River
London, England
Saturday, June 16
1:15 p.m.**

Occasionally Colophon would catch a brief glimpse of
sunlight filtering down through a drain. But for the
most part, their journey was dark and cold. An entire
city lay just above her head, she knew, yet she had
never felt more isolated from the rest of the world.
Everything was strange and unfamiliar. The air
felt stale and undisturbed. Every step she took and

every sound she made echoed down the long brick passageway. Wide round tunnels and small narrow ones ran off in all directions. Some of them seemed to plunge almost straight down. She wondered how deep they went, and if anyone had ever dared venture down there—or perhaps more important, whether anything from down there ever ventured up. On a couple of occasions they passed through large chambers, the ceilings of which rose to twenty feet or more. At one bend in the passageway they encountered a series of mysterious iron rings attached to the wall. Try as he might, Julian could not come up with a reasonable explanation for them.

And she could hear things. Things that scraped, skittered, and scratched just outside the beam of her flashlight.

It was all very disquieting.

For the first twenty minutes or so, she pestered Julian constantly about how far they had traveled. He patiently responded on each occasion—and she was always surprised by how far they still had to go. She finally quit asking and walked in silence.

It seemed as if they had been walking forever when he suddenly stopped. She looked up ahead. They were about to enter another big chamber.

"This is it," he said. "One mile."

They stepped into the large brick chamber. Their steps echoed high into the darkness above. Colophon swept her flashlight across the room. Just like the other chambers they had passed through, this one gave off to several smaller tunnels. However, something about this round central chamber struck her as different. The room had a symmetry that the previous chambers lacked. The ledge on which she and Julian stood continued around the entire chamber and formed a complete circle. She counted three tunnels on each side of the room. They were all identical—tall with arched entrances. They looked barely wide enough for one person to walk through at a time. And there was something else. Above each tunnel was a brass medallion. Even in the faint illumination provided by her flashlight, she could tell that something was engraved on each medallion.

And then she pointed her flashlight at the chamber's ceiling.

"Look!" she exclaimed.

Stars made of bronze and set into the brick swirled around the ceiling. On one side was a large brass sun. On the other was a crescent moon.

"Magnificent," Julian said. "Do you have any doubt we're in the right place?"

"None," Colophon said.

She looked out over the chamber. "Miles's symbol —the sigma—must be on the medallion over one of the tunnels."

"You take the right side," said Julian as he headed to the left.

Colophon crossed over a small brick bridge to the right and came to the first tunnel. She stood on her toes and looked at the medallion. The engraving wasn't a sigma, but it was an image she knew—a hawk holding a spear. It was identical to the image in the book that Julian had found in Wales.

"It's not this one!" she yelled. "But we're getting close!"

From across the room, Julian called, "It's not this medallion. It's an engraving of an inkwell."

Colophon moved to the next tunnel. The medallion over its entrance contained an image of a pair of crossed quills. Engraved on the medallion over the final tunnel was a lily—identical to the image on the crest for Corpus Christi College. All the symbols were familiar—but they weren't the right one.

She met Julian on the far side of the chamber. "Any luck on your side?"

"No," he replied. "An inkwell, a pelican, and a key —but not the symbol we're looking for."

She sat down on the ledge that ringed the chamber. "I'm confused. It's clear that this is where Miles Letterford intended for us to be—but where's the symbol? We can't just head down each tunnel."

Julian paced up and down the ledge. "I'm missing something. And it's right here in front of us—I just know it is."

"You haven't missed anything," she said. "The hidden message said the sigma symbol would be here—one mile north of the Thames. But it's not."

Julian stopped in his tracks and turned back to her. "No, that's not what the message said. It didn't say anything about a symbol—it's what we interpreted it to say. How could I have been so stupid?"

"What do you mean? The symbol isn't here?"

He grinned broadly. "No, but the mark is."

"The mark—the symbol—what's the difference?"

Julian pulled off his bag and set it on the ground. He reached inside and pulled out a book. It was the Christopher Marlowe book that he had found in Wales.

"We're supposed to be looking for the mark," Julian said. "A printer's mark."

"What's a printer's mark?"

"It was a stamp in a book—a mark used to identify who printed it. Different printers used different marks. The mark was usually placed at the end of the book."

He opened the book to the last page and showed it to Colophon. It was a design that she had seen hundreds of times before—a crescent moon over crossed quills.

"It's the Letterford family crest," she said. "My grandfather used to have it on his stationery."

Julian nodded. "And it was the printer's mark used by Miles Letterford."

Colophon pointed her flashlight up at the tunnel medallion engraved with crossed quills. She slowly moved the light directly up the wall until it illuminated a large brass object directly above that particular tunnel—the crescent moon.

Julian laughed. "It's ironic, isn't it?"

"What's ironic?" she asked.

"Don't you know what a printer's mark is also called?"

Colophon was confused. What was he talking about? And then it hit her. She did know. She had known since she was a small child. How could she have missed it?

"A printer's mark," she finally replied, "is also called a colophon."

CHAPTER THIRTY-FIVE

Remorseless

Remorseless — Having no pity or
compassion; merciless.

Fleet River
London, England
Saturday, June 16
1:30 p.m.

"A colophon!" she repeated.

"Yes," Julian said. "All along we've been looking
for the colophon. Do you think Miles Letterford could

ever have envisioned that the person who made it this far would be you?"

Colophon paused. The thought gave her chills. But what happened next made her blood run cold.

"Congratulations," said a deep voice from across the chamber. The word lingered heavily in the darkness.

Julian swung his flashlight around and pointed it in the direction of the voice. "Treemont!"

Treemont stood at the far end of the chamber. "Congratulations are in order," he said. "This is quite an accomplishment."

"What are you doing here?" Julian demanded. Colophon could hear the nervousness in his voice.

"Securing what is rightfully mine," Treemont replied.

"You have no right to be here!" Colophon yelled. "You stole the company from my father!"

Treemont smiled. "Your father has no idea of the true legacy of Miles Letterford." He pointed his own flashlight at Julian. "And as much as it pains me to say it, this buffoon was the only member of the family who even had a clue."

"I thought you didn't believe in the treasure," Julian said.

"Believe?" said Treemont. "Believing is for philosophers and priests. I knew the treasure existed."

"But how?" Julian asked.

"My father, of course," said Treemont.

"Your father worked for Letterford and Sons his whole life," Julian said. "He was a good man. If he knew about the treasure, he would have told the family about it. He never would've helped you steal the family business."

"My father wasted his life working for Letterford and Sons. He treasured his role as the records keeper. He was a fool. But just before he died, he found a rather unique book in the archives of the company. The book was accompanied by a note from Miles Letterford—a note detailing instructions for the printing of two such books. My father believed in the treasure and was convinced that the books held the key." Treemont paused. "Of course, he entrusted his only son with the book and the note. I assured him they would be delivered to your grandfather."

"But you didn't," Colophon said.

"Of course not," Treemont replied. "But my father was right—the books held the key."

Julian looked down at the book he held in his hands. "Two books?"

"Yes," said Treemont. "Two books—virtually identical—the same binding, the same decoration on the cover, and the same unique engravings on the inside."

"Virtually identical?" Colophon said. "What was the difference?"

Treemont reached under his jacket and pulled out a leather-bound book. He handed it to Julian.

Julian examined the book. It was identical to the book he had discovered in Wales—with one exception.

"It's another play," said Julian.

"By Marlowe?"

"No," Julian said. "*Richard the Second* . . . by William Shakespeare."

Colophon was confused. What did this mean? One play by Marlowe and the other by Shakespeare?

"It appears," said Julian, "that the books were intended to serve . . . as guides of some sort."

Colophon could hear the uncertainty in his voice.

"I'm not exactly sure why there are two books," he continued, "but I suspect the answer lies at the end of that tunnel."

Treemont pointed his flashlight at the medallion with the crossed quills and then at the crescent moon on the ceiling. "There's only one way to find out," he said.

"There's no way we're going to help you," Julian said. He gestured to Colophon. "We need to leave."

"But what if the treasure is in there?" she pleaded. "We can't leave. Even if Treemont inherits everything, at least it'll prove my dad's not a liar."

Julian paused. He looked down at the book in his hand—the very book that his ancient ancestor had left to serve as a guide to whatever was located in this tunnel bearing the family crest. He knew he had to continue. "Okay," he finally said, bending down to retrieve his bag. "Let's go."

Treemont stepped into the tunnel and out of view. "Are you coming?" he called back to them.

Julian whispered to Colophon, "Be careful. Don't get too close to Treemont."

Julian followed Treemont into the tunnel. Just as he did, Colophon heard a sickening thud. Julian crumpled to the ground. Blood trickled down the side of his face. Treemont stood over him, holding his heavy metal flashlight like a club.

"You killed him!" she screamed.

"He's not dead . . . yet," Treemont replied. He grabbed Colophon by the arm. She was surprised by the strength of his grip. "Into the tunnel. You might still prove useful."

Colophon started walking. Treemont's footsteps

followed close behind. She scanned the walls and the floor as she walked, looking for a side passageway that might provide a means of escape from Treemont —but the tunnel offered no such avenue. The flashlight in her hand was plastic and lightweight, hardly a weapon of significance, and she had nothing in her backpack that would help. Her only option was to keep moving forward.

Water dripped and drained into the tunnel from pipes on the walls. Steam whistled from vents in the ceiling. The temperature increased dramatically. The air was heavy and stale. Cobwebs draped thickly across the tunnel, and she could not see more than a few feet ahead.

The tunnel seemed to go on forever.

Chapter Thirty-Six
Misgiving

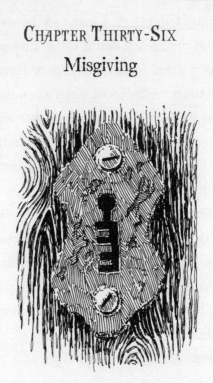

Misgiving—Doubt, distrust, or apprehension.

Colophon was exhausted.

Sweat poured down her face. Cobwebs clung to every part of her body. Her feet were soaked and sore. She wanted to turn around and tell Treemont that they must have taken the wrong tunnel.

She desperately wanted to go back and check on Julian.

And she wanted to go home.

Why had she not listened to Julian? He had warned her that this could be dangerous.

And then the tunnel just stopped.

In front of her was a large wooden door. Bolted in the middle of the door was a large round brass plate, and etched on the plate was a single image—Σ. The door had no other ornamentation, just a lock with a single keyhole. She realized immediately that there was only one key in the world that would open the lock. The key that Treemont now possessed as owner of Letterford & Sons.

"This is it." He pushed past her.

He pulled the key from his pocket, held it up, and examined it with his flashlight. She could see the familiar symbol of the sigma engraved on it. The same symbol that she and Julian had discovered in the mausoleum in Stratford. The same symbol that had been on the box containing the Shakespeare manuscripts. The same symbol in the portrait of Christopher Marlow. It was a symbol, Colophon recognized, that represented much more than she had ever expected.

Treemont placed the key in the lock and turned it. There was a soft click, followed by the sound of metal bolts sliding back into the wall. The door opened ever so slightly, and a small hiss of air escaped. He pulled on the handle and the large door slowly creaked open. A blast of air blew into the tunnel. Cobwebs fluttered behind them.

Treemont stepped into the room.

Colophon could see his flashlight flicking back and forth.

"It's magnificent!" he proclaimed. "The Letterford treasure at last!"

London, England
Saturday, June 16
2:05 p.m.

Colophon stepped through the doorway. To her surprise, the room was cool, and the air fresh.

The light from her flashlight offered only small, tantalizing glimpses of the interior. But Treemont was right—the room was magnificent. It appeared to be long and relatively narrow. She could see the walls to her left and right; the far end of the room eluded her flashlight's beam. The high walls were lined with bookcases—all filled to the brim with books as far as she could see into the darkness. She pointed her flashlight up. The ceiling was made of brick—like the tunnels—and arched high. From it hung a wooden chandelier filled with candles. She could make out the faint silhouettes of more chandeliers hanging from the middle of the ceiling. She pointed her flashlight toward the center of the room and saw a huge table filled with objects of various sizes and shapes. The items glinted and gleamed as the beam passed over them.

"You won't get away with this," Colophon said. "The family will find out what you've done."

The voice was now within a few feet of where she stood. "But I've already gotten away with it—with the exception of one loose end."

She turned her flashlight in his direction. Treemont stood between her and the doorway. She had nowhere to go. She threw her flashlight at him, but it missed and clanked across the brick floor.

He pointed his flashlight at her, and the bright light blinded her. She could hear his footsteps coming closer, but she couldn't see him. She balled up her fists. Treemont was at least a foot taller and outweighed her by a hundred pounds. But she was prepared to fight, scratch, and claw with every ounce of strength she had.

The footsteps came closer.

And then they stopped.

Treemont towered above her. She stared up at his cold dark eyes.

"And now," he said, "we've come to the end of our little quest."

Her heart pounded. She told herself to fight back but felt paralyzed with fear. Her arms and legs wouldn't move. She closed her eyes.

This is it, she thought.

CHAPTER THIRTY-SEVEN

Sanctimonious

Sanctimonious —Smugly or
hypocritically righteous.

London, England
Saturday, June 16
2:25 p.m.

And then . . . nothing.

Colophon opened her eyes in time to see Treemont's
flashlight spinning off into the darkness. The light
flickered from one wall to the next. She could hear
scuffling and made out the silhouettes of two people,
but she couldn't tell what was happening.

Someone else was in the room, but who? Was it Julian?

WHACK.

Something heavy hit the floor in front of her.

And then came the voice.

"DON'T TOUCH MY SISTER!"

A flashlight clicked on. Colophon could see Treemont lying on the floor, his glasses hanging from the side of his face. Standing above him was Case. She had forgotten how much her brother had grown over the last year—he looked more like a man than a teenage boy.

Treemont started to get up, his eyes filled with rage.

Suddenly a large, furry missile exploded from the darkness and landed on Treemont's chest. He fell backwards to the ground.

"Maggie!" Colophon cried. The golden retriever glanced at Colophon and offered a quick wag of her tail, then, growling with teeth bared, turned her attention back to Treemont.

Colophon rushed over to Case and hugged him. For once, she had no words for her brother.

"For the record," said Case, "searching for clues in a sewer qualifies as doing something stupid."

Colophon nodded. She tried to keep her composure, but the tears were flowing. "What about Mom and Dad?" she asked.

"I had to leave before they got home," Case replied. "We're on our own."

"Did you see Julian?" Colophon asked. "He was hurt."

"I'll survive," Julian said as he stepped into the room. His clothes and bag were soaked, he had a large knot on the side of his head, and he smelled like a sewer. "A raging headache—but it could've been worse."

Case turned to Treemont. "You'll pay for this," he said.

Treemont looked up at Case. "Pay for what? Your sister came down here of her own accord. I found Julian unconscious back in the sewer and came looking for her. She's lucky I found her. I was simply trying to help her get back home."

"That's a lie," Julian said. "You knocked me out and forced her down here."

"The clumsy fool must have slipped and fallen," Treemont continued, ignoring Julian.

"You were going to hurt me," Colophon said, "until Case showed up."

"A misunderstanding," Treemont replied. "Nothing more. Now, I suggest you get your dog off me before I have you arrested for trespassing and assault."

Case whistled for Maggie, who reluctantly backed away from Treemont and stood at her owner's side.

Treemont stood, dusted himself off, and straightened his glasses. "Shameful is what it is. A young girl running around in a sewer with her miscreant cousin. And then her brother and his dog assault me as I'm trying to help the poor girl."

"You were following us," insisted Julian.

"I was searching for what is rightfully mine," Treemont replied. He bent over, picked up his flashlight, and pointed it at the table in the middle of the room. "And I found it."

Chapter Thirty-Eight

Design

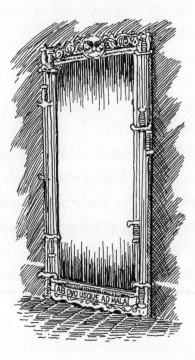

Design—A reasoned purpose; an intent.

London, England
Saturday, June 16
2:35 p.m.

Julian removed a box of matches from his bag, stood on a chair, and carefully lit the ancient candles in the chandelier hanging in the middle of the chamber. A large mirror at the far end reflected the light back throughout the room, bathing it in a warm amber glow.

Case, Julian, Colophon, and Treemont stood around the table.

It was remarkable.

The table was filled with artifacts, manuscripts, and objects that defied imagination and, in many instances, description. Julian pointed to a large book bound in a brilliant red lambskin. "A pristine edition of Shakespeare's First Folio," he marveled. He turned to Colophon. "It's the first printed collection of Shakespeare's plays. Almost four hundred years old and in perfect condition!"

Colophon peered at a small, oddly shaped object on the table. *Is that a silver nose?* she wondered.

But of all the objects on the table, one item almost immediately seized everyone's interest.

"Look," said Julian. He pointed to a small, nondescript journal on the table's edge. On the cover was an image of a falcon holding a spear. And beneath this image was a single initial and a single word: W. SHAKESPEARE. Everyone stood transfixed by the sight.

Julian picked it up and wiped the thick layer of

dust from its cover. He then gently skimmed through the pages.

All discussion ceased. The room fell silent save for the gentle whisper of the pages as they turned. Finally, Julian closed the journal.

"Well?" said Treemont.

"It is," said Julian, "exactly what it appears to be —the journal of William Shakespeare."

"Yes!" said Colophon.

"And," he continued, "it unquestionably authenticates the Shakespeare manuscripts that we discovered—the handwriting is identical."

Colophon looked at her brother. "The manuscripts are real."

Case nodded. He was trying to stay composed, but she could see the relief in his eyes. The last few weeks had been difficult for both of them.

"So now I own both Shakespeare's journal and his manuscripts," said Treemont. "This has proven to be quite a momentous day."

"There's more," said Julian, ignoring him.

Again the room fell silent.

"The journal," he said, "appears to have been written during Shakespeare's lost years."

Colophon turned to him. "What are you talking

about? What lost years? You never mentioned any lost years."

"It's one of the enduring mysteries of Shakespeare," said Julian. "He just sort of disappeared from Stratford in 1582 and then reappeared a decade later as an actor and playwright in London. There's very little evidence as to what he did during those years — until now." Julian paused. "It appears that Shakespeare traveled quite extensively through Europe — often in the company of a reputed spy."

"Christopher Marlowe!" Colophon exclaimed.

Julian smiled. "Marlowe indeed."

"Wait a second," said Colophon. "Does that mean Shakespeare was also a spy?"

"That remains to be seen," replied Julian. "But the objects on this table and throughout this room were apparently collected by Marlowe and Shakespeare on their trips throughout Europe. I suspect the stories preserved in this journal were never meant to be revealed in their lifetimes. It appears Shakespeare trusted only one man to preserve those stories — Miles Letterford. Can you imagine what can be learned from this journal?"

"What can be *learned?*" Treemont said. "That

book is worth tens of millions of dollars — and it's mine. The highest bidder can do with it as they like."

Colophon stepped back from the table. She wondered if the room held more clues.

She turned and looked at the large mirror at the far end of the room. It was as if she were looking through a window into another world. She walked slowly toward the mirror until she stood directly in front of it.

It was huge and ornate. It towered over her. Carved into the top of the mirror's frame was a large medallion with the heads of two bearded men facing in opposite directions. The sides of the frame had been carved to resemble swords. And at the bottom of the frame — carved into an open scroll — were the words AB OVO USQUΣ AD MALA.

A slight smile crossed Colophon's face.

"Something funny?"

She turned to find Julian standing beside her. At the far end of the room she could see her brother arguing with Treemont. Case seemed to be holding his own.

Colophon pointed to the words at the bottom of the frame. "He never lets up, does he?" she said.

"Who?" asked Julian.

"Miles Letterford," she replied. "More Latin—another clue."

Julian sighed. "Not this time, I'm afraid. I believe that inscription is there for a very specific purpose. It's an old Roman saying—it means 'from eggs to apples.'"

"From eggs to apples? You don't think that's mysterious?"

"No. The ancient Romans ate their meals in a specific pattern—literally from eggs to apples. It's the same as saying from beginning to end."

Colophon stared at the inscription. "So it means this is truly the end."

"And, I suppose, the beginning as well," Julian said. "Miles Letterford probably used this room to plan his clues. This is where it all started."

"And so this is where it all ends," she replied.

Colophon stared into the mirror.

"So no more clues," she said.

"I'm afraid not," Julian replied. "We've come full circle."

She pointed at the top of the mirror. "So is that what the two-headed guy is supposed to represent?"

"Yes, that's the Roman god Janus. He was the god

of beginnings and endings. He was represented by . . ." Julian paused in midsentence. He stared up at the two-headed man.

"What?"

"It's probably nothing," he said. "It's just that Janus was also the god of . . . doorways."

"The god of doorways?"

Julian didn't respond. He simply stared at the mirror.

"What are you thinking?" Colophon asked.

Instead of replying, Julian walked over to the mirror and ran his hands down each side and across its surface. He put his ear against the glass and listened. He then bent down and examined the inscription at the bottom of the frame.

Colophon knelt beside him and watched Julian run his finger across the inscription.

AB OVO USQUΣ AD MALA

From eggs to apples.

Julian's finger lingered over the third word. Then Colophon realized what he was looking at—the last letter in the word was not an E, it was Σ.

Sigma.

Julian looked at Colophon, grinned, and pushed down on the letter.

✦ ✦ ✦

At the opposite end of the room, Treemont continued to argue with Case. "This chamber belongs to me," he said. "You and your sister and Julian need to get out."

Case was furious. Treemont was right—they couldn't prove that he had attacked Julian or that he intended to harm Colophon. And technically, the room and its contents belonged to Treemont—that is, until the family found out the manuscripts were real. Maybe. For now, Case knew he needed to get Colophon back home—and get Julian checked out by a doctor.

"We're leaving," Case said.

He turned to call his sister, when—

CLANK

The sound reverberated through the room.

CLANK CLANK CLANK

"It's Colophon and Julian," said Case. He pointed at the opposite end of the room. "The mirror—it's moving!"

Treemont looked toward the far end. To his amazement, the mirror was opening—like a large door.

Colophon and Julian stood back as the mirror slowly opened. They could hear large gears turning somewhere deep within the wall—metal against metal.

CLANK CLANK CLANK CLANK CLANK

Colophon looked into the opening behind the mirror. At first, all she saw was darkness. But to her amazement, light slowly filled the space, revealing a set of stone stairs behind the mirror. The light, she realized, was coming not from within the chamber but from some unseen source at the top of the stairway.

Suddenly Maggie ran past her and bounded up the stairs.

"Maggie!" Colophon yelled. But it was too late—Maggie was gone.

Colophon started after Maggie, but Julian grabbed her. "Wait. You don't know what's up there."

"Maggie's up there!" she insisted. "I've got to go after her!"

She broke from Julian's grasp and headed for the stairs.

"Stop!" The deep voice brought her to an immediate halt.

It was Treemont. He was walking directly toward her. "I've had enough of you and your cousin," he said. "Turn around and leave—now!"

Treemont reached Colophon and stepped between her and the stairway. "Have you gone deaf? I said leave!"

But Colophon was no longer paying any attention to Treemont. Nor was Julian or Case.

A large shadow on the stairway behind Treemont had grabbed everyone's attention—a shadow with two arms, two legs, and a head.

Treemont, oblivious, continued to berate Colophon until, finally, the shadow spoke.

"Hello?"

The voice came from the top of the stairway and caught Treemont by surprise. He jumped out of the doorway and behind Julian.

"Hello?" the shadow repeated.

Colophon stepped toward the shadow. "Mom?"

"Coly? Is that you?" the voice answered.

A moment later Meg Letterford appeared in the doorway, immediately joined by Mull.

"Mom! Dad!" Case exclaimed. "What are you doing here?"

"What are *we* doing here?" Meg said. "The better question is, what are you doing here? I was in the kitchen trying to reach you on your cell phone when suddenly Maggie came running in to greet us. All I know is that we have a set of stairs where the fireplace in our library used to be."

"Our library?" said Colophon. She turned to Julian. "You mean the Letterford treasure has been under our house the whole time?"

"Wait a second," said Mull Letterford. "What treasure? What's going on?"

Colophon pointed toward the table in the middle of the room. "Dad, it's the real Letterford treasure. We found it!"

"Mull," said Julian, "the Shakespeare manuscripts were just the beginning. This room will change history!"

Treemont's voice cut through the room and stopped any further discussion. "Enough!" he said. "Get out— all of you."

"Now see here," said Mull Letterford. "I think an explanation is in order."

Treemont looked at Mull. "The only explanation is that you're trespassing."

Colophon turned to Treemont. "We're not trespassing. And we're not leaving."

Treemont's eyes turned cold. "I've warned you."

"There's a trespasser here," said Colophon, "but it's not us."

She pointed up at the library. "Remind us—who owns the house at the top of the stairs?"

The blood drained from Treemont's face.

"I can answer that," said Julian. "I believe Mull Letterford is the rightful owner of the home. Isn't he, Treemont?"

Treemont opened his mouth, but nothing came out.

Julian stood directly in front of Treemont. "I trust you understand what this means."

"This can't be," Treemont exclaimed. He held up the Letterford family key. "The key is mine!"

"I'm not exactly sure what's going on," said Meg Letterford, "but I know one thing. That key might belong to you, but this room is part of our house." She poked her finger into the middle of Treemont's chest. "And unless you want to be arrested for trespassing, I suggest you leave immediately."

Treemont glared at Meg. "You wouldn't."

Meg glared back at Treemont. "It would be my great pleasure," she replied.

Colophon could see the uncertainty in his eyes. "This won't stand," he muttered as he started up the stairs.

"Hold on," said Mull. "Where are you going?"

Treemont looked confused. "I'm leaving."

"I don't know how you got in here," Mull replied, "but you need to leave the same way."

Case pointed at the door leading back into the sewer. "I believe it's that way."

"You can't be serious," said Treemont.

"I am very serious," said Mull.

Treemont walked to the far end of the room and stood at the door to the sewer. "Just wait! The family will never stand for this!"

But the battle was over, and Treemont knew it. No one had to respond. The Letterford family stood and stared at him. Treemont picked up his flashlight, turned, and reentered the tunnel without another word.

CHAPTER THIRTY-NINE
Unreal

Unreal — So remarkable as to
elicit disbelief; fantastic.

London, England
Saturday, June 16
3:05 p.m.

Mull Letterford looked at Colophon and Case. "Without you, I never would have believed that the treasures in this room existed."

"Don't forget Julian," said Colophon. "He always believed."

"Even when the rest of us did not," said Mull. He walked over to Julian and shook his hand. "I know I'm in no position to ask this, but I was hoping that you could help me with the next task."

"Anything," said Julian.

"I need someone I trust to oversee the cataloging of this room," Mull replied. "And I trust you."

For once Julian was at a loss for words.

"Of course he will," said Colophon. "He's perfect for the job."

"It would be an honor," Julian finally replied.

Colophon and Julian sat on the stairs and watched Mull and Meg Letterford as they examined the table of treasures. There was an ornately decorated clock, a large jeweled saber, a glass ball filled with powder, a silver stamp, a tall hourglass, a stack of brightly colored manuscripts, a golden chalice, a broken dagger, a mummified hand under a glass dome, and numerous other oddities.

It didn't seem real. After all this time, they had finally discovered the true family treasure.

She sighed.

"You don't look excited," Julian said.

"I am excited," she replied. "It's just . . . well . . . aren't you kind of sad that it's all over?"

"I know what you mean. I've spent most of my life looking for this room, and now here it is."

"There's one thing I can't figure out," said Colophon. "Why did Treemont do it? Why did he try to ruin my family?"

Julian paused and collected his thoughts. "The stuff in this room is worth millions of dollars, but I don't think it was really about money for Treemont. Shakespeare said it best—a 'savage jealousy.' Treemont always resented your father. It consumed him."

Colophon nodded. That made sense, knowing Treemont. Whatever his reasons, she hoped it was the last time she had to deal with him.

She put her head on Julian's shoulder. "Just remember to call me if you uncover any more mysteries," she said. "You're absolutely helpless without me."

Epilogue

"Good evening," Richard Brayson said directly to the camera, "and welcome to CNN's *Newsmakers*. I'm coming to you live from London, England."

The camera panned to reveal Mull Letterford standing next to Brayson in the chamber beneath the Letterford home.

"Tonight we are speaking with Mull Letterford, recently reinstalled as the owner of Letterford and Sons, about the discovery of a vast treasure trove of ancient artifacts, books, and manuscripts beneath his home in London."

Brayson turned to Mull. "Mr. Letterford, thank you for joining us this evening."

"My pleasure," replied Mull.

"If you would," said Brayson, "tell us what it felt like the first time you entered this room."

"It was quite an experience," replied Mull. "I imagine it was how Howard Carter must have felt when he discovered—"

Click.

"My pleasure," replied Mull.

"If you would," said Brayson, "tell us what it felt like the first time you entered this room."

"It was quite an experience," replied Mull. "I imagine—"

Click.

"It was quite an experience," replied Mull. "I imagine—"

Click.

"It was quite an experience," replied Mull. "I imagine—"

Click.

Hadley Musselman muted the video. He was tired of listening to Brayson and Letterford ramble on about the room. He had watched the video of Mull Letterford's interview a hundred times or more. It didn't matter what Brayson or Letterford said. It was simply background noise. The only thing that mattered was an object on the corner of the table behind Letterford. He had glimpsed it fleetingly—it had appeared for only a brief moment when Letterford turned ever so slightly, at the beginning of the interview. But that was enough.

Musselman paused the video.

There it was. There was no question.

He picked up the phone and dialed his client's number.

"It exists," he said into the phone, "and I've found it."

"Are you sure?" the voice on the other end replied. "You know, last time —"

"To be present, but not seen," Musselman said. "Is that enough proof for you?"

There was a long pause on the other end of the line. Musselman grinned. This little discovery would pay a few bills — and then some.

"Yes," the voice finally said. "That's enough."

FINI

Author's Note

William Shakespeare did not simply use the English language—he twisted it, manipulated it, and bent it to his will. And when the perfect word was not to be found, he simply created one to suit his particular need or modified the meaning and use of an existing one. It seems remarkable (and incredibly audacious) that a writer would simply invent a word or change the way a word is used or understood. And yet Shakespeare did just that—time and time again.

The chapter titles in this book are words that Shakespeare is believed to have invented—or for which his works represent the first known usage. A list of the chapter titles and the works in which these words first appeared are set forth in the appendix.

The prologue to Part 2 is a brief quote from *As You Like It,* a comedy believed to have been written by William Shakespeare in approximately 1599. Some scholars believe that this quote is a direct reference by Shakespeare to the murder of Christopher Marlowe. Marlowe is believed to have died in a "little room"—Elanor Bull's Public House—over the matter of a "reckoning"—that is, dividing up the bill for food and drink at the end of the day.

Appendix

CHAPTER 1. Auspicious—*Hamlet*
act 1, scene 2
King Claudius:
> Have we, as 'twere with a defeated joy,
> With one *auspicious* and one dropping eye,
> With mirth in funeral and with dirge in marriage,
> In equal scale weighing delight and dole,
> Taken to wife: nor have we herein barr'd
> Your better wisdoms, which have freely gone
> With this affair along.

CHAPTER 2. Exposure—*Troilus and Cressida*
act 1, scene 3
Nestor:
> Makes factious feasts; rails on our state of war,
> Bold as an oracle, and sets Thersites—
> A slave whose gall coins slanders like a mint—
> To match us in comparison with dirt;
> To weaken and discredit our *exposure,*
> How rank soever rounded in with danger.

CHAPTER 3. Pedant—*The Taming of the Shrew*
act 3, scene 1
Hortensio:
> But, wrangling *pedant,* this is
> The patroness of heavenly harmony:

Then give me leave to have prerogative;
And when in music we have spent an hour,
Your lecture shall have leisure for as much.

CHAPTER 4.   Hint—*Othello*
act 1, scene 3
Othello:
Wherein of antres vast and desarts idle,
Rough quarries, rocks and hills
whose heads touch heaven
It was my *hint* to speak, such was the process.

CHAPTER 5.   Perusal—*Hamlet*
act 2, scene 1
Ophelia:
He took me by the wrist and held me hard;
Then goes he to the length of all his arm,
And, with his other hand thus o'er his brow,
He falls to such *perusal* of my face
As he would draw it.

CHAPTER 6.   Luggage—*King Henry IV, Part I*
act 5, scene 4
Prince Henry:
Come, bring your *luggage* nobly on your back:
For my part, if a lie may do thee grace,
I'll gild it with the happiest terms I have.

CHAPTER 7.   Fitful—*Macbeth*
act 3, scene 2
Macbeth:
Duncan is in his grave;

After life's *fitful* fever he sleeps well;
Treason has done his worst: nor steel, nor poison,
Malice domestic, foreign levy, nothing
Can touch him further.

CHAPTER 8. Instinctively—*The Tempest*
act 1, scene 2
Prospero:
In few, they hurried us aboard a bark,
Bore us some leagues to sea; where they prepar'd
A rotten carcass of a boat, not rigg'd,
Nor tackle, sail, nor mast; the very rats
Instinctively have quit it: there they hoist us,
To cry to the sea that roar'd to us; to sigh
To the winds whose pity, sighing back again,
Did us but loving wrong.

CHAPTER 9. Accused—*King Henry VI, Part II*
act 1, scene 3
Horner:
God is my witness, I am
falsely *accused* by the villain.

CHAPTER 10. Amazement—*The Tempest*
act 5, scene 1
Gonzalo:
All torment, trouble, wonder, and *amazement*
Inhabits here: some heavenly power guide us
Out of this fearful country!

CHAPTER 11. Mimic—*A Midsummer Night's Dream*
act 3, scene 2
Puck:

Anon his Thisbe must be answered,
And forth my *mimic* comes. When they him spy,
As wild geese that the creeping fowler eye,
Or russet-pated choughs, many in sort,
Rising and cawing at the gun's report,
Sever themselves, and madly sweep the sky,
So, at his sight, away his fellows fly;
And, at our stamp, here o'er and o'er one falls;
He murder cries, and help from Athens calls.

CHAPTER 12. Gossip—*The Comedy of Errors*
    act 5, scene 1
    Duke Solinus:
        With all my heart, I'll *gossip* at this feast.

CHAPTER 13. Puke—*King Henry IV, Part I*
    act 2, scene 4
    Prince Henry:
        Wilt thou rob this leathernjerkin, crystal-button,
        knot-pated, agate-ring, *puke*-stocking, caddis-garter,
        smooth-tongue, Spanish-pouch,—

CHAPTER 14. Questioning—*As You Like It*
    act 5, scene 4
    Hymen:
        Whiles a wedlock hymn we sing,
        Feed yourselves with *questioning*,
        That reason wonder may diminish,
        How thus we met, and these things finish.

CHAPTER 15. Gnarled—*Measure for Measure*
    act 2, scene 2
    Isabella:

Nothing but thunder. Merciful Heaven!
Thou rather with thy sharp and sulphurous bolt
Split'st the unwedgeable and *gnarled* oak
Than the soft myrtle.

CHAPTER 16.   Nervy—*Coriolanus*
act 1, scene 1
Volumnia:
Death, that dark spirit, in 's *nervy* arm doth lie;
Which, being advanc'd, declines, and then men die.

CHAPTER 17.   Rumination—*As You Like It*
act 4, scene 1
Jaques:
I have neither the scholar's melancholy, which is
emulation; nor the musician's, which is fantastical;
nor the courtier's, which is proud; nor the
soldier's, which is ambitious; nor the lawyer's,
which is politic; nor the lady's, which is nice; nor
the lover's, which is all these: but it is a
melancholy of mine own, compounded of many simples,
extracted from many objects, and indeed the sundry
contemplation of my travels, which, by often
rumination, wraps me in a most humorous sadness.

CHAPTER 18.   Gloomy—*King Henry VI, Part I*
act 5, scene 4
Joan La Pucelle:
May never glorious sun reflex his beams
Upon the country where you make abode;
But darkness and the *gloomy* shade of death

Environ you, till mischief and despair
Drive you to break your necks or hang yourselves!

CHAPTER 19.   Dishearten—*King Henry V*

act 4, scene 1:

King Henry V:

Therefore when he sees reason of fears, as we
do, his fears, out of doubt, be of the same relish
as ours are: yet, in reason, no man should possess
him with any appearance of fear, lest he, by showing
it, should *dishearten* his army.

CHAPTER 20.   Vulnerable—*Macbeth*

act 5, scene 8

Macbeth:

Let fall thy blade on *vulnerable* crests.

CHAPTER 21.   Discontent—*King Henry VI, Part II*

act 3, scene 1

King Henry VI:

Ay, Margaret; my heart is drown'd with grief,
Whose flood begins to flow within mine eyes,
My body round engirt with misery,
For what's more miserable than *discontent*?

CHAPTER 22.   Viewless—*Measure for Measure*

act 3, scene 1

Claudio:

To be imprison'd in the *viewless* winds,
And blown with restless violence round about
The pendant world.

CHAPTER 23. Multitudinous—*Macbeth*

act 2, scene 2

Macbeth:

> Whence is that knocking?
> How is't with me, when every noise appals me?
> What hands are here! Ha! they pluck out mine eyes.
> Will all great Neptune's ocean wash this blood
> Clean from my hand? No, this my hand will rather
> The *multitudinous* seas incarnadine,
> Making the green one red.

CHAPTER 24. Dawn—*King Henry V*

act 4, scene 1

King Henry V:

> Not all these, laid in bed majestical,
> Can sleep so soundly as the wretched slave,
> Who with a body fill'd and vacant mind
> Gets him to rest, cramm'd with distressful bread;
> Never sees horrid night, the child of hell,
> But, like a lackey, from the rise to set
> Sweats in the eye of Phoebus and all night
> Sleeps in Elysium; next day after *dawn*,
> Doth rise and help Hyperion to his horse,
> And follows so the ever-running year,
> With profitable labour, to his grave.

CHAPTER 25. Denote—*Romeo and Juliet*

act 3, scene 3

Friar Laurence:

> Thy wild acts *denote*
> The unreasonable fury of a beast.

CHAPTER 26.   Dauntless—*King Henry VI, Part III*
act 3, scene 3
King Lewis XI:
> Yield not thy neck
> To fortune's yoke, but let thy *dauntless* mind
> Still ride in triumph over all mischance.

CHAPTER 27.   Ode—*Love's Labour's Lost*
act 4, scene 3
Dumain:
> Once more I'll read the *ode* that I have writ.

CHAPTER 28.   Eyeball—*The Tempest*
act 1, scene 2
Prospero:
> Go make thyself like a nymph of the sea: be subject
> To no sight but thine and mine; invisible
> To every *eyeball* else. Go, take this shape
> And hither come in't: go, hence with diligence!

CHAPTER 29.   Excitements—*Hamlet*
act 4, scene 4:
Hamlet:
> How stand I then,
> That have a father kill'd, a mother stain'd,
> *Excitements* of my reason and my blood,
> And let all sleep?

CHAPTER 30.   Engagements—*Julius Caesar*
act 2, scene 1
Brutus:

Hark, hark! one knocks. Portia, go in awhile;
And by and by thy bosom shall partake
The secrets of my heart.
All my *engagements* I will construe to thee,
All the charactery of my sad brows.
Leave me with haste.

CHAPTER 31.   Negotiate—*Much Ado About Nothing*
act 2, scene 1
Claudio:

Let every eye *negotiate* for itself
And trust no agent; for beauty is a witch
Against whose charms faith melteth into blood.

CHAPTER 32.   Stealthy—*Macbeth*
act 2, scene 1
Macbeth:

Now o'er the one half-world
Nature seems dead, and wicked dreams abuse
The curtain'd sleep; witchcraft celebrates
Pale Hecate's offerings, and wither'd murder,
Alarum'd by his sentinel, the wolf,
Whose howl's his watch, thus with his *stealthy* pace.

CHAPTER 33.   Forward—*King Henry VI, Part II*
act 3, scene 2
Salisbury:

And mere instinct of love and loyalty,
Free from a stubborn opposite intent,
As being thought to contradict your liking,
Makes them thus *forward* in his banishment.

CHAPTER 34. Premeditated—*King Henry VI, Part II*

act 3, scene 1

Bishop of Winchester:

Com'st thou with deep *premeditated* lines,
With written pamphlets studiously devis'd.

CHAPTER 35. Remorseless—*King Henry VI, Part II*

act 3, scene 1

King Henry VI:

Thou never didst them wrong, nor no man wrong;
And as the butcher takes away the calf
And binds the wretch, and beats it when it strays,
Bearing it to the bloody slaughter-house,
Even so, *remorseless*, have they borne him hence.

CHAPTER 36. Misgiving—*Julius Caesar*

act 3, scene 1

Cassius:

I wish we may: but yet have I a mind
That fears him much; and my *misgiving* still
Falls shrewdly to the purpose.

CHAPTER 37. Sanctimonious—*Measure for Measure*

act 1, scene 2

Lucio:

Thou concludest like the *sanctimonious* pirate, that
went to sea with the Ten Commandments, but scraped
one out of the table.

CHAPTER 38. Design—*The Tempest*

act 1, scene 2

Prospero:

> Out of his charity,—who being then appointed
> Master of this *design*,—did give us; with
> Rich garments, linens, stuffs, and necessaries,
> Which since have steaded much.

CHAPTER 39. Unreal—*Macbeth*

act 3, scene 4

Macbeth:

> What man dare, I dare:
> Approach thou like the rugged Russian bear,
> The arm'd rhinoceros, or the Hyrcan tiger;
> Take any shape but that, and my firm nerves
> Shall never tremble: or be alive again,
> And dare me to the desart with thy sword;
> If trembling I inhabit then, protest me
> The baby of a girl. Hence, horrible shadow!
> *Unreal* mockery, hence!

— COLOPHON —

THUS ENDS THIS BOOK:

A Tale of the Letterford Family

BY DERON R. HICKS.

✣

PRINTED BY HOUGHTON MIFFLIN HARCOURT,
AND FIRST OFFERED TO THE DISCERNING PUBLIC
ON THE EIGHTH DAY OF OCTOBER, MMXIII.
THE TEXT FONTS ARE NEW CENTURY SCHOOLBOOK, EUPHORIGENIC, AND CAPTAIN KIDD.

— ✣ —

with great thanks & appreciation to the following:

AGENT: STEVEN CHUDNEY
PUBLISHER: BETSY GROBAN
EDITORIAL DIRECTOR: MARY WILCOX
EDITOR: ANN RIDER
EDITORIAL ASSISTANT: AMY CHERRIX
MANAGING EDITOR: MARY HUOT
COPYEDITORS: JANET BIEHL AND ALISON KERR MILLER
PROOFREADER: TONI ROSENBERG
ART DIRECTOR: CAROL CHU
ASSISTANT DESIGNER: SUSANNA VAGT
PRODUCTION MANAGER: DIANE VARONE
JACKET ILLUSTRATOR: GILBERT FORD
INTERIOR ILLUSTRATOR: MARK EDWARD GEYER
MARKETING MANAGER: LISA DISARRO
PUBLICIST: RACHEL WASDYKE

✣ ✣ ✣

Read the first book in
the Shakespeare Mysteries series!

A JUNIOR LIBRARY GUILD SELECTION

"The combination of humor and suspense works well to keep readers turning the pages of this modern-day mystery." —*Kirkus Reviews*

"An entertaining debut." —*Publishers Weekly*

"A fine traditional mystery with a modern sensibility." —*Booklist*

"Superbly written [and with], plenty of action, a bright and inquisitive 12-year-old girl protagonist, and lots of literary flair, this book can be recommended to pretty much any kid in the 8–13 range." —*Decatur Metro*

"A ripsnorting, stylish mystery with an appealing but unlikely pair of puzzle-solving detectives." —*Booksforkids* blog